LITTLE WARRIOR

❀

GIUSEPPE CATOZZELLA

Translated by Anne Milano Appel

❀

FABER & FABER

First published in the UK in 2016
by Faber & Faber Ltd
Bloomsbury House
74–77 Great Russell Street
London WC1B 3DA

First published in the USA as *Don't Tell Me You're Afraid*
by Penguin Press, 375 Hudson St, New York, NY 10014

Printed and bound by CPI Group (UK) Ltd, Croydon CR0 4YY
Text designed by Marysarah Quinn

Published by arrangement with Agenzia Santachiara
First published as *Non dirmi che hai paura* in January 2014 by Giangiacomo Feltrinelli
Editore, Milan, Italy

A CIP record for this book
is available from the British Library

ISBN 978-0-571-32268-8

FSC
www.fsc.org
MIX
Paper from
responsible sources
FSC® C101712

2 4 6 8 10 9 7 5 3 1

CONTENTS

❊

CHAPTER 1

※

THE MORNING THAT Alì and I became brother and sister was hot as blazes, and we were huddled under the skimpy shade of an acacia.

It was Friday, a holiday.

The run had been long and tiring, and we were both dripping with sweat: from Bondere, where we lived, we'd come straight to the CONS (Somali National Olympics Committee) stadium in Mogadishu without once stopping. Seven kilometers, making our way through all the side streets, which Alì knew like the back of his hand, under a sun scorching enough to melt stone.

Our combined age was sixteen: We were both eight years old, born three days apart. We couldn't help but be brother and sister, Alì was right, even if we were from two families who weren't even supposed to talk to each other yet lived in the same house, two families who had always shared everything.

We were under that acacia to catch our breaths a little and cool down, covered up to our behinds with the powdery white dust that swirls up from the roadbeds at the slightest puff of wind, when all of a sudden Alì came out with that bit about being his *abaayo*.

"Wanna be my *abaayo*?" he asked me, his breath still ragged, hands on his bony, narrow hips in the blue shorts that had been worn by all his brothers before ending up on him. "Wanna be my sister?" You know someone all your life, yet there is always one exact moment from which point on, if he is important to you, he will always be a brother or sister.

Bonded for life by a word, you remain that way.

I looked at him sideways, not letting him know what I was thinking.

"Only if you can catch me," I said abruptly, before taking off again, back toward our house.

Alì must have given it everything he had, because after a few strides he managed to grab me by my T-shirt and make me stumble. We ended up on the ground, him on top of me, in the dust that clung everywhere, to the sweat on our skin and to our thin clothing.

It was almost lunchtime. There was no one around. I didn't try to squirm free, didn't put up any resistance. It was a game.

"Well?" he asked, his breath hot on my face as he suddenly became serious.

I didn't even look at him, just squeezed my eyes shut, disgusted. "You have to give me a kiss if you want to be my brother. Those are the rules, you know."

Alì stretched out like a lizard and pressed a big wet kiss on my cheek.

"*Abaayo*," he said. Sister.

"*Aboowe*," I replied. Brother.

We got up and took off again.

We were free, free to run again.

At least as far as the house.

Our house wasn't even a house in the normal sense of the word, not like those nice ones with all the comforts. It was small, very small. And two families lived in it, mine and Alì's, around the same courtyard enclosed by a low earthen wall. Our dwellings faced each other from opposite sides of the yard.

We were on the right and had two rooms, one for me and my six brothers and sisters and the other for our mother and father. The walls were a mixture of mud and twigs, which hardened in the sun. Between our two rooms, as if to separate us from our parents, was the room belonging to the landlords: Omar Sheikh, a big fat man, and a wife even fatter than him. They had no children. They lived near the coast, but every so often they came to spend the night there, and when that happened the days immediately became much less pleasurable. "Save your jokes and funny stories for the day after tomorrow," my oldest brother, Said, would say whenever he saw them coming, referring to when they would leave again.

Alì, however, with his father and three brothers, lived in only one room, alongside the wall to the left.

The best part of the house was the courtyard: a huge enclosure, I mean really huge, with an enormous, solitary eucalyptus. The yard was so big that all of our friends wanted to come to our place to play. The ground, like the floor inside the house and everywhere else, was the usual fine white dust that in Mogadishu ends up all over the place. In our bedroom, for example, we'd laid straw mats under the mattresses, but they didn't help much: Every two weeks Said and Abdi, my older brothers, had to take them outside and beat them as hard as they could, trying to get rid of every single grain of sand.

The house had been built by the fat man, Omar Sheikh, himself many years earlier. He'd wanted it put up right around the majestic eucalyptus. Having passed by it every day since he was a child, he'd come to love that tree, or so he told us countless times in that ridiculous little voice of his, which came out breathless. At that time the eucalyptus was already tall and sturdy, and he had thought: *I want my house to be here.* Then, under the dictator Siad Barre's regime, business problems had arisen and it seemed that war was coming, so he'd decided to move to a more peaceful location and had rented the three rooms to our two families, mine and Ali's.

At the back of the yard was the shed that served as the communal toilet: a tiny cubicle enclosed by dense bamboo canes, with a nauseating central hole where we did our business.

On the left, just before the latrine, was Ali's room. On the right, facing it, was ours: four by four meters, with seven mattresses on the floor.

Our brothers slept in the center and we four girls slept beside the walls: Ubah and Hamdi on the left and Hodan, my favorite sister, and I on the right. In the midst of us all, like an unfailing, protective hearth, stood the inevitable *ferus*, the kerosene lamp without which Hodan would never have been able to read and write her songs late into the night, and Shafici, the youngest of the boys, would not have been able to perform his hand-shadow plays on the wall; the figures were so clumsy and ungainly that they made us die laughing. "You create great entertainment out of shadows and a lot of imagination," Said told him.

All in all, the seven of us tucked into that little room had loads of fun before going to sleep each night, trying not to let our mother and father hear us, or Yassin, Alì's father, who slept across the way from us with Alì and his three brothers. A few steps away from me. Alì and I had been born three days apart and were separated by just a very few steps.

Since we'd come into the world, Alì and I had shared food and the outhouse every day. And of course dreams and hopes, which come with eating and shitting, as *aabe*, my father, always said.

Nothing ever separated us. Alì for me was always like a boy version of Hodan, and Hodan a graceful Alì. We three were always together, just the three of us; our world was complete; there was nothing that could separate us, even though Alì is a Darod and I'm an Abgal, the clans that have been at war since eight weeks before we were born, in March 1991.

Our mothers gave birth to us, the lastborn, while the clans gave birth to war: our "big sister," as my mother and father always said. An evil sister, yet someone who knows you perfectly, who knows very well how easy it is to make you happy or sad.

Living in the same house, as Alì and I did, was forbidden. We were supposed to hate each other, the way the other Abgal and Darod hated each other. But no. Instead we always did things our own way, including eating and shitting.

The morning that Alì and I became brother and sister we were training for the annual race through the districts of Mogadishu. It was two weeks away, and to me that seemed like an eternity. Race day was the most important day of the year for me. Friday was a holiday and there was also a curfew in effect, so you could go around freely and run through the streets of the city, surrounded by all that whiteness.

Everything is white in Mogadishu.

The walls of the buildings, riddled by bullets or nearly demolished by bombs, are almost all white, or gray or ocher or yellowish; in any case, light colored. Even the poorest dwellings, like ours, made of mud and brushwood, soon become white like the dust of the streets, which settles on the facades as on everything else.

When you run through Mogadishu, you raise a cloud of fine, sandy powder behind you. Alì and I created two white trails that very slowly vanished toward the sky. We always ran the same route; those streets had become our personal training field.

When we ran past the rundown bars where old men sat playing cards or drinking *shaat*, tea, our dust would end up in their glasses. Every time. We did it on purpose. Then they'd pretend to get up to run after us, and we'd speed up and leave them behind in no time, raising still more dust.

It had become a game—we laughed and the old men laughed a little too. We had to be careful where we stepped, however, because at night they burned the garbage and the next morning the streets were littered with charred remains. Gas cans, oil tins, shreds of tires, banana peels, broken bottles, anything you can think of. In the distance, as we ran, we could see scores of smoldering heaps, countless little erupting volcanoes.

Before slipping into the narrow alleys leading to the big street that hugged the coast, we always went along Jamaral Daud, a broad two-lane boulevard with the usual dusty surface and a row of acacia trees on either side.

We loved to run by the national monument, the parliament, the national library, the courthouse. Lined up in front of the complex were the street vendors, their colorful cloths spread out on the ground, displaying their wares: everything from tomatoes and carrots to windshield wipers. The men dozed beneath the trees lining the boulevard until a customer showed up, and when we ran by they looked at us as if we were a couple of martians. They made fun of us.

"Where are you two rascals going in such a hurry? It's a holiday. Have fun, take it easy," they called as we sped past.

"Home to your wife, you old sleepyhead!" Alì replied. Sometimes they threw a banana at us, or a tomato or an apple.

Alì would stop, pick them up, and then sprint away.

The race was an event. To me it seemed like it was even more important than July 1, our national holiday, the day we declared independence from Italian colonizers.

As usual, I wanted to win, but I was only eight years old, and everyone was participating, even the adults. At the race the year before I'd finished in eighteenth place, and this time I wanted to cross the finish line in the top five.

When my father and mother saw me so motivated, from the time I was little, they tried to figure out what was going through my head.

"Will you win again this time, Samia?" Aabe Yusuf, my father, teased me. Sitting in the courtyard on a woven straw chair, he pulled me to him and ruffled my hair with those huge hands of his. I enjoyed doing the same thing to him, running my short, skinny little fingers through that thick black mane or pounding his chest through the white linen shirt. Next he would grab me and, big and strong as he was, lift me up in the air with only one arm, then set me back down on his lap.

"I haven't won yet, Aabe, but I will soon."

"You look like a fawn, you know that, Samia? You're my favorite little fawn," he'd say then, and hearing his big deep voice become tender made my knees tremble.

"Aabe, I'm swift *as* a fawn, I'm *not* a fawn. . . ."

"So tell me. . . . How do you think you can win against those kids who are bigger than you?"

"By running faster than them, Aabe! Maybe not yet, but someday I'll be the fastest runner in all of Mogadishu."

He would burst out laughing, and if my mother, Hooyo Dahabo, was nearby, she too would laugh out loud.

But right after that, while he was still holding me tight, Aabe would become melancholy. "Someday, of course, little Samia. Someday . . ."

I tried to convince him. "You know, Aabe, some things you just know. I've known since before I could talk that someday I'll be a champion. I've known since I was two years old."

"Lucky you, my little Samia. I, however, would just like to know when this damn war will end."

Then he put me down and went back to staring straight ahead, his face grim.

CHAPTER 2

❀

THE WAR NEVER MATTERED much to me and Alì. Let them shoot each other in the street; it had nothing to do with us. Because the war couldn't take away the only thing that was important: what he was to me and what I was to him.

War can take away other things, but not that. For example, it took the sea away from me. The first thing I smelled when I was born was the smell of the sea, which traveled straight from the coast all the way to the courtyard of the house, the saltiness that still clings to my hair and skin, the moisture that permeates every molecule of air.

Yet I touched the sea only once. I know it's water, that if you jump into it you'll get all wet, like when you go to the well, but until I do it I don't believe it.

Sometimes I touched the sand, even though I shouldn't have. Every now and then Alì and I, taking our time as we ran through the narrow alleys that only he knew, would approach the sea's vast expanse in the afternoon. We'd stop at the side of the big road that runs from north to south along the entire length of the shoreline and, hidden behind a truck or an armored tank, would stay there for hours watching the waves move back and forth, teasing the sunlight that reflected everywhere. We were dying to dive in. That immensity was there in front of our eyes and we couldn't go in it.

Once or twice, however, Alì became impatient. I could tell by the way he kept rubbing his hands together without letting up. He looked around, took me by the arm, and told me to run. Just that one word: "run." Those times we crossed the big road and sat on the sand. Crazy! They could shoot us: The beach is one of the militia's favorite spots; it's wide open; the rifles' bullets have a straight shot.

But we'd pretend we were normal kids who didn't think about such things and could just play.

The sand was hot and fine like specks of gold. We didn't see a soul nearby. We started tussling around, trying to get the sand all over each other, in our black curly hair, in our clothes, everywhere. After he rolled me over two or three times, Alì laughed like a madman; he looked like a lunatic. I had never seen him like that. He opened his mouth and displayed his big white teeth, saying, "You look like a meatball covered with corn flour!" and he went on laughing with that funny face of his: flat nose, big fleshy lips and small, close-set little eyes.

"You're a corn flour–covered meatball!" he repeated.

I tried to squirm free but I couldn't; he was too strong for me, even though he had no muscles: tall as a string bean and all bones. He kept me pinned on the sand while I tried to wriggle loose, pretending he wanted to kiss me on the mouth as he leaned forward, stretching his head out like a turtle. I turned my face right and left, disgusted, but when he got close, instead of kissing me Alì said "Boo!" and blew sand in my eyes.

I hated him.

One time, only once, gripped by a power greater than us, we slowly approached the water. One small step after another, almost without realizing it.

It was a beautiful expanse, gigantic, like a sleeping elephant breathing deeply. The long waves made an amazing whoosh that resembled a voice; they sounded like the small shells in the glass jar that Aabe had given Hooyo when they were engaged, which she kept hidden in a wooden cabinet in their room. We would go pick up the jar and turn it over slowly from one side to the other to hear the voice of the sea.

Shhhh. Shhhh.

We moved closer and dipped our hands and feet in the water. I stuck my fingers in my mouth. Salty.

That night, after that approach, I dreamed about waves. I dreamed of losing myself in that vastness, letting it cradle me, drifting up and down according to the water's mood.

Well, war, as I said, took the sea away from me. But on the other hand, it made me want to run. Because my desire to run is as deep as the sea. Running is my sea.

In any case, if Alì and I always pretended that the war didn't exist, it's because we were the children of Yusuf Omar, my father, and Yassin Ahmed, Ali's father. They too have been friends since the day they were born, and they too grew up together in the village of Jazeera, south of the city. They attended the same school and their fathers also worked together, in the period of the Italian colonists. Together our two fathers learned some proverbs in that language from their two fathers. *Non fare oggi quello che puoi fare domani*, "Don't do today what you can do tomorrow." And *Tutto il mondo è paese*, "The world is the same wherever you go."

Aiutati che Dio t'aiuta, "God helps those who help themselves."

Another saying they learned from them is *Cascassero sulla tua testa mille chili di merda molle molle*, "May a thousand pounds of runny shit fall on your head," with all its variants, which was a phrase their fathers' Italian boss always used to say, back when they worked at the port, unloading containers. One day a container packed with manure had suddenly opened up and the boss had been inundated by that "rain" from above. Since then things had gone very well for him, but even so he'd started using that expression whenever he felt like swearing.

Another proverb said, *Siamo tutti figli della stessa patria*, "We're all children of the same country." This one is a favorite of Aabe and Yassin: best friends whom nothing will ever come between.

Like us.

"Can anything ever break us apart?" Alì and I wondered on those sweltering, brutally hot afternoons when he helped me climb the eucalyptus and we took shelter in the coolness of the leaves for half a day, talking about the future. Staying up there in the eucalyptus was wonderful; in place of the real world, we concocted one in which only we two and our dreams existed.

"No!" we told each other in turn. And then we made the gesture swearing to be blood brothers: We kissed our linked index fingers in front of our mouths twice, reversing right and left. Nothing and no one could come between us. We would have bet anything, even our lives.

But that eucalyptus was also Alì's favorite spot where he went to hide by himself. For example, in the afternoon when he didn't want to learn to read.

Although Hodan was five years older than me, in fact, every morning she and I went to school together, to the Madrasa Musjma Institute, a district comprising primary, middle, and secondary classes. Alì didn't come with us; his father never had the money to allow him to study. He attended first grade at the public institution, but then the school was destroyed by a grenade and he hasn't gone back since then. After that unhappy day classes were held outdoors, and it wasn't easy to find teachers willing to risk a bomb on their heads.

The only way to learn was to enroll at the private school. Our father was able to afford it for a few years, thanks to many sacrifices, whereas since the beginning of the war Yassin has always had trouble selling his fruit and vegetables.

In Mogadishu it was said that few people wanted to buy from a filthy Darod.

Alì has always been touchy about the fact that we knew how to read and write. It made him feel inferior. His clan was in effect viewed that way in our neighborhood, and that was one of the things that proved it.

Every now and then we tried to teach him the letters of the alphabet, but after a while we gave up.

"Alì, try to focus," Hodan told him; she's always had a tendency to act like a schoolmarm, a little mother.

He tried hard, but it was too difficult. Learning to read was a long process; you couldn't attempt it in the afternoon, sitting in the courtyard at a small table that Aabe and Yassin used for playing cards, under a sun that was still hot and made you want only to have fun. The only one who experienced anything like fun was Hodan, who played the teacher and made me and Alì be her pupils. I was always the good student, and he was the one who didn't pay attention.

"I can't," Alì would say. "It's too hard. Besides, I don't care about learning! Being able to read is useless!"

I had to play the part of the schoolmate who wanted to help him; otherwise Hodan would get mad. "Come on, Alì. It's not so difficult; even I learned how. Look, these are the vowels: *a, e, i, o* . . ." I tried to encourage him.

He'd run away. It was hopeless. He'd stick it out for ten minutes until Hodan, at the beginning of the class, started reading a passage from a book. When it was his turn to try to read, he made up any excuse to disappear. Those times, when Hodan insisted and made him angry, Alì would climb the eucalyptus and stay there.

His eucalyptus. His favorite spot.

One afternoon, after arguing with his brother Nassir, he climbed up to the top and stayed there for almost two days. No one was able to get him to come down; no one else could climb all the way up there. Nassir tried every way he could to persuade him, but there was no way. Alì came down only the second night, weakened by hunger.

After that we started calling him "monkey." Only a monkey like him could make it up there to the top. He'd rather be called that than learn how to read.

Anyway, Alì always acted uppity, but he was slower than me, even if he was a boy. He was stronger—if we fought he beat me—but he was slower.

When he wanted to make me angry, he said I was a *wiilo*, a

tomboy, and that was the only reason I ran so fast. He said I was a boy who'd been born in the body of a girl, that I was a know-it-all snot nose just like the boys, and that when I got big I'd grow whiskers like his father, Aabe Yassin. I knew it; there was no need for him to tell me: I knew I was a tomboy and that when people saw me running without veils, without the *qamar* and the *hijab*, wearing only shorts and a T-shirt bigger than I was, since I was thinner than an olive branch, they thought that I was not a perfect daughter of the Koran.

But in the evening, after supper, when the adults enjoyed making us compete in the courtyard for a scoop of sweet sesame paste or a chocolate *angero*, a crepe, I showed him. The courtyard was the center of life for all families; with the war it was best to leave the house as infrequently as possible.

After Hooyo Dahabo, with the help of my sisters, had cooked supper for everyone on the *burgico*, the brazier as big as a whole cow, and after we had finished eating what there was—usually bread and vegetables or rice and potatoes, and every once in a while a little meat—Aabe Yusuf and Aabe Yassin prepared the track for us.

Our older brothers and sisters cheered while Alì and I, posed like champions, bent over at the starting line, crouching down with our hands on the ground. We even had starting blocks, which Aabe had built by taking apart two wooden watermelon crates.

For the lines that marked the lanes, Said and Nassir, our older brothers, had to drag their feet from the end of the courtyard to the earthen wall, about thirty meters, outlining a turnaround and tracing a course back to the starting point.

I always won.

Alì hated me, but in the end I almost always shared the thing I love most in the world, my sweet sesame, with him—there's nothing I love more than sweet sesame paste. But first I'd make him promise not to call me *wiilo* anymore. If he agreed, I gave him half.

On those summer evenings, when the air finally cooled down a little, after the races Hodan and I would play *shentral*. Those were beautiful, relaxing days, when we all forgot about the war. *Shentral* was played by drawing a bell on the ground and then writing the numbers one to nine in it. You tossed a pebble and it had to land on the bell. Our brothers were playing *griir* instead, sitting on the ground and making stones fly between their hands.

Every now and then on those drawn-out, breezy evenings, Ahmed, a friend of Alì's big brother Nassir, would join us. Ahmed was seventeen, like Nassir and Said. To me and Alì he seemed very grown up, and to me and Hodan he looked handsome and unattainable. Ahmed had an olive complexion and light eyes, uncommon in Somalia; those green eyes gleamed in the moonlight and made his gaze seem all the more bold.

Once we asked him why his eyes were different from everyone else's; he made the gesture of having sex—one hand forming a circle while his index finger moved in and out—and told us that his grandfather must be one of the Italians who had fooled around with the black girls. Nassir and Alì burst out laughing. Not my brother Said; he gave him his usual stern look and shook his head.

Said didn't get along well with Ahmed, unlike Nassir, who idolized him. Maybe he saw him as a rival because of his friendship with Nassir, or maybe he just didn't like him; he always had misgivings about him, saying that there was something in those light eyes that he didn't trust. Alì never got too close to Ahmed either. He often stared at him, studying him, but he kept away from him. Usually, when Hodan and I played *shentral*, Alì stayed near his father and Aabe, who argued every night at cards, staring at Ahmed cautiously from a distance.

Some nights, after *griir* or playing ball, Ahmed and Said ended up scuffling, sometimes joking around and other times for real, and Aabe and Yassin would have to pull them apart. Once Said punched Ahmed so hard that blood spurted from his nose and stained his white T-shirt. He looked like he'd been hurt badly.

After a while Aabe made them shake hands, and the next night, as if nothing had happened, they were friends again.

One of the nicest things about those summer nights, however, was Hodan singing.

Often, after Hooyo and we girls had finished washing the pots, we would all sit in a circle for hours, listening to her velvety voice transform familiar tunes.

Aabe and Yassin sat smoking, their languid eyes turned to the sky, and I wondered what a big, handsome man like Aabe could be asking the stars. Every now and then my sisters and I and Hooyo, moved by Hodan's words, would wipe our eyes and noses with our handkerchiefs; the older brothers and Ahmed sat in the dust, arms hugging their legs, staring at the ground.

Once in a while Ahmed looked up, and those icy green eyes flashed in the moonlight; he seemed to want to defy the moon. When he did that I turned my head away and brought my focus back to the face of Hodan, who, seated in the center, her eyes half closed, went on singing songs about peace and freedom.

CHAPTER 3

❋

THE NIGHT BEFORE the annual race, before our fathers came home from work, Alì and I did a forbidden thing: We ventured out to run.

It was six o'clock in the afternoon, the sun was low on the horizon, and the smell of the sea drifted right into the courtyard. Driven by a fresh breeze that was redolent with aromas beginning to rise from the braziers of the neighboring houses, the sea's scent had seeped in and drawn us to it. There were only a few hours left before the race and we wanted to stretch our muscles and lengthen our strides. We felt a need to, like two real athletes.

Often the militia decided to have the curfew begin in the hours preceding Friday. That evening, in fact, no gunshots could be heard. Then too there was a full moon, enough light that it wasn't too risky.

We wouldn't go very far.

We set off with the idea of going around the block, as far as avenue Jamaral Daud, turning around at the national monument, then heading back.

Twenty, twenty-five minutes in all.

Alì had told me to put on the veils, but I hadn't listened to him. Hooyo—who was bent over a steaming pot, cooking, wrapped in the gauzy white veils she wore around the house—hadn't even noticed that we were going out. Nor had Hodan, inside the room with our other sisters.

Making as little noise as possible, we sneaked under the red curtain covering the opening in the boundary wall, sure that no one would spot us.

The war didn't scare us; it was our "big sister."

Often, when mortar strikes or machine-gun shots were heard, Alì and his friends Amir and Nurud would go up close to the militiamen to see how they fired. They crept up ever so slowly and hid behind a car or around the corner of a house and watched. The sound of rifles, of machine guns, excited them. When they came back to the courtyard, they talked a mile a minute, and I stood there gaping, listening to them; talking over one another, each of them wanted to tell me about a detail that he thought only he had seen. Their eyes were lit up, fiery as the opening of a rifle barrel.

Anyway, that night we ran for about twenty minutes. The air was cool and we didn't get sweaty like during the day. That was the hour I liked; everything had slowed down, the day was drawing to a close, and instead of the afternoon's blinding sunlight a suspended glow hovered in the air, the sun's rays bouncing everywhere, reflecting off every particle of dust, but lower, more restful.

We were already on our way back, not too far from home,

when we were forced to stop. Suddenly, at the end of a deserted alley, a jeep carrying fundamentalist militiamen appeared.

They were neither Hawiye nor Abgal nor Darod but members of Al-Shabaab, an Islamist militant group.

Ethnicity in this case had nothing to do with it. They were militants backed by extremists of Al-Qaeda who were doing everything they could to seize power, taking advantage of the divisions among the clans.

The Al-Shabaab men were recognizable from a distance by their long beards and dark jackets. Unlike the clans' militiamen, who usually wore camouflage jackets they'd recovered from some market or obtained secondhand from the Ethiopian army, the soldiers of Al-Shabaab wore real uniforms, new ones, which made them look like rich warlords.

There were eight men in the truck bed, the barrels of their machine guns sticking up from behind their backs like metal antennas.

The jeep was moving very slowly when one of the bearded men turned his head toward us and saw us coming.

Two harmless little specks, tired and sweaty.

A half-naked little Abgal girl and a Darod boy with a flat nose and ebony black skin.

The man banged his fist on the roof of the cab, and the jeep stopped. Everything happened in a few seconds. Two militiamen jumped down and came toward us.

They were short and had no beards.

Only when they got close did we realize why: They were young boys, twelve, maybe eleven years old. Sporting rifles bigger than they were over their shoulders. At that time it was rumored that Al-Shabaab had started recruiting children to teach them about holy war. In return, they guaranteed the parents that their children would receive an education, learn Arabic and the laws of the Koran, be fed three meals a day, and sleep in decent housing, with a real bed and all the comforts that almost no one could afford anymore. Those two must be new recruits.

The closer they came, looking at me disapprovingly, the more aware I became of how I was dressed: shorts and a T-shirt. Damn it! The veils. And Alì was Darod, one of the clans the fundamentalists hated the most because they considered them inferior, a clan of niggers, as they said, while we Abgal had lighter, amber-colored skin and features more closely resembling those of the Arabs, from whom the Al-Shabaab extremists liked to think they were descended.

They stopped about twenty paces from us.

"What are you two doing out and about at this hour?" said the shorter, chubbier one of the two, in his nicely ironed black shirt and creased dark trousers. In our minds a nearly perfect outfit like that pertained only to Europe or America. We were used to dressing any old way, in hand-me-down clothes. Only a few adults loved to parade around on Fridays, in the square by the parliament or along the seaside promenade, wearing the same pants and jackets they'd worn during the years of peace.

"We're training for the race tomorrow," Alì replied, looking boldly at him, unafraid. The questions were routine. Though it had never happened to us, there were numerous stories of similar incidents going around; there was nothing to fear from those questions.

The two burst out laughing, the fat one scratching his behind with one hand. Then they took a few steps forward, and the solitary streetlight lit up their faces. Their eyes were watery and bloodshot.

"So you're both athletes. . . ." the fat one said after a pause, his tone ironic as he started laughing again.

"Right," Alì replied. "We're training for the annual race. . . ."

At that point, the other one, a lanky kid with a long scar on his forehead and eyes that looked possessed, yelled: "Shut up, Darod! Don't even open your mouth. I could take you away, you know, and no one would say a word about it. Maybe your father would even be happy if you came with us. At least you'd have some decent clothes to wear." They burst out laughing again like little children, while the chubby one continued scratching his backside.

Alì lowered his eyes and looked at himself. He wore a T-shirt riddled with holes and food stains, which had been his brother Nassir's, and a pair of shorts way too big for him, held up at the waist by a string. On his feet were a holey pair of moccasins that his father, Yassin, had salvaged somewhere, who knows how many years ago.

Out of the corner of my eye I sensed movement.

Alì was shaking like a drum skin. He was sobbing silently out of anger and shame. I turned around and saw a tear, just one, roll down his cheek.

Like a predator sniffing around a wounded animal, the skinny one with the scar came five or six steps closer. He wore a men's cologne with a penetrating odor, like Acqua di Colonia, but too strong; it hung in the air around us.

"You're just a dirty little Darod," he said. "Remember that. You're just a filthy Darod."

Alì didn't answer. I was scared.

Then Scarface came up to me and grabbed me by the arm. "And maybe we'll take your little friend away. That'll teach her to dress like a *wiilo*. What do you think you are, huh? A boy?"

I tried to wriggle free, but he kept a tight grip on me, like claws. He tried to drag me, but I resisted, digging my heels into the ground.

All of a sudden Alì exploded and, like a cat, pounced on the kid's hand and bit it. Scarface let go of my arm and Alì gave me a shove, shouting at me to run home.

I looked at him, not knowing what to do. I didn't want to leave him there alone, but I knew we needed help.

The skinny one kept waving his hand in the air as if to dry it and wipe away the teeth marks; rather than getting back at Alì for the bite, he smiled, his expression ominous. Then he said: "Hey, this Darod is gutsy."

The fat one stopped scratching himself, nodded, and with the same hand smoothed back a strand of hair.

"You've got balls, Darod," he said. "Who's your father?"

"It's none of your business who my father is, fatso," Alì replied.

"Well, if we can't talk with whoever should have taught you good manners, then we'll have to take you in the jeep. . . ." They came up and grabbed him under his arms. Alì tried to shake them off, but there were two of them and they were bigger than him.

"Maybe some of the adults might like to teach you good manners, Darod. And to be smarter. It's not smart to bite someone who's carrying a gun. . . ."

While Alì continued to struggle and I stood there petrified, a third man got out of the jeep.

In the dim light you could see that he was much taller than them; he must have been older, but he too had no beard. Maybe he was still young. Maybe he was reasonable.

He approached us and told the two to release the Darod. "Let him go. Get in the jeep. I'll take care of him."

Alì and I turned to that shadow. We had recognized the voice.

Together we looked up at his face.

He was maybe five yards away from us. The streetlamp gave off little light, but the icy green eyes that flashed, though clouded by the same strange watery film as those of the two kids, were his.

Ahmed.

Nassir's friend, with whom Hodan was secretly in love.

The two boys muttered something and reluctantly let Alì go.

When they reached the jeep, Ahmed said in a soft, low voice, so he wouldn't be heard by his companions: "Be careful, you two. Going out alone is dangerous."

Then he turned on his heel and signaled the driver to restart the engine.

Before jumping into the jeep bed, as the vehicle was already moving, he stared at Alì with an ominous expression. A split second that seemed like an eternity.

The green eyes glinted in the moonlight. That look made my blood run cold. A mixture of pleasure and promise. It was not a challenge, just an air of insidious alliance.

Then, as slowly as it had arrived, the Al-Shabaab soldiers' jeep moved off again.

I was shaking like a leaf. Alì, instead, was all worked up.

"Damn fundamentalists! That's all we needed in this city; it's not enough that we have all those other armed groups!" he burst out.

Such inspection checks could happen, of course, but it was better to hear about them from other people's stories. I went over to hug him and try to calm him down, but he pushed me away.

"I'm okay. Leave me alone. Those filthy extremists didn't do a thing to me," he muttered without even looking at me, staring at the ground.

"Those two had something about their eyes that seemed unnatural. . . ." I said.

"Of course. They were all high on khat," Alì replied.

A pause.

"What's khat?"

"It's that filthy narcotic that Al-Shabaab gives its soldiers."

"They get high and then go around shooting?"

"No. It's *so that* they will then go around shooting that they give it to them. They offer it to the young ones, so they'll become addicted."

"They seemed lost, as if they were possessed by an evil spirit," I said to myself, hoping the feeling would quickly pass.

As if he'd been lost in thought, Alì came back. "That fat one kept scratching his ass."

"He must have had ticks in his briefs, never mind the new clothes." I smiled.

"Yeah, in fact, that shitty ass of his must have been full of ticks. . . ." he said, laughing. He turned to look off toward the spot where the jeep had been stopped shortly before, as if to make sure that it was really gone.

I took his hand and this time he didn't pull away.

Slowly we made our way back home, spouting one silly thing after another. We went all the way without ever mentioning Ahmed.

In the courtyard Hooyo, sitting on a chair, was still stirring, bent over the steaming pot heated by the brazier. She had covered her hair with a white veil, which she avoided wearing at home when she wasn't cooking.

Seen from the entrance, the skin of her face—illuminated by the moon and firelight and beaded with drops of moisture from the steam—seemed very smooth. Firm and shiny like the rind of a watermelon at noon.

Just for a change, that night we ate rice and vegetables.

CHAPTER 4

❊

THE NEXT MORNING we ran the race.

The gathering place was at the national monument at eleven o'clock; the sun was almost at its peak and it was hot as hades.

The course wound through the streets of the city to the stadium: Once we entered it, we would run a lap around the field, then cross the finish line.

There were three hundred of us. For twelve months it was all I'd been waiting for: Week after week, day after day, I had mentally retraced every meter, every curve; I had imagined every moment of the race, picturing myself entering the stadium and at the finish.

Still, last night's encounter with Ahmed, along with Alì's mood, had had an effect on me too.

So I wasn't able to give what I could have. I tried to keep to the edge of the group, I did everything I'd planned to do, but something inside me didn't respond as I had expected. A part of my brain kept thinking about the glitter of those icy green eyes when they looked at Alì.

A year. I had spent a year training and I wasn't able to give my best. I would never forgive myself.

The course was the usual one; Alì and I had run it a thousand times. The streets had been cleared of the few cars that normally traveled them and knots of vendors were gathered along the entire length of Jamaral Daud, selling water or refreshing juices, bananas and chocolate bars for a few shillings. With its trash cleared away, the avenue was unrecognizable.

Had it been any other day, I could have won.

But no. I came in eighth.

Alì finished one hundred and forty-ninth.

"You're better at biting than running," I teased him afterward. He had also ended up in a pool of excrement: an open sewer. Realizing that he was behind, he had cut through a side street where trash and feces were dumped at night, ever since a bomb had ruptured the sewer system built by the Italians. The cesspool that day had spread over the entire width of the street. Alì had thought it was shallow but found himself in it up to his calves. Still, he had gained a lot of ground.

At home that night we celebrated.

Hooyo cooked kebabs of lamb tripe and entrails, which I was crazy about. *Kirisho mirish*, a spicy meat and rice dish, along with sweet sesame paste, was my favorite. We were happy; Aabe told a lot of jokes and made us all laugh.

Alì, on the other hand, ashamed of the stench that stuck to him, didn't even want to come out of his room. His brother Nassir had made him wash before going in, and afterward he refused to come out.

Every so often, when Said or Nassir called out, teasing him about the stink, Alì shouted something from the room, sniveling woefully. At that point we all chimed in.

"Leave me alone!" he yelled from his self-imposed isolation.

"Go on, come out and eat, Stinko!" Nassir kept at him, knowing he was making him even angrier.

"No, I'm never eating with you again," Alì shouted.

"May a thousand pounds of sewage fall on your head," Said piped up, and we all laughed uproariously. Alì didn't answer.

Something was bothering him.

The fact that Ahmed was one of the fundamentalists' militiamen had affected him deeply.

I'd told him that my brother Said was right not to trust Ahmed, but Alì had replied that Nassir was very close to Ahmed, so he couldn't be bad.

Since that day, however, his eyes would suddenly cloud over with sadness now and then.

I'd try to make him laugh, but he would soon lapse back into his reflections.

I didn't know what to do.

After that night, for several weeks he began to spend more and more time up in the eucalyptus. If we played *griir*, he got confused about the number of pebbles and lost; and he had always beaten all of us. When we played hide and seek, he always hid in the same places, and if someone pointed it out to him, he paid no attention. He didn't care about winning.

He stayed up in his dumb eucalyptus, thinking about who knows what.

I didn't recognize him anymore.

One afternoon, out of the blue, he told me that he was going to stop running and that he would become my coach.

"Why the heck should you be my coach?" I asked him as I laced up my shoes.

"You're faster than me. It's pointless for me to keep trying. I don't have an aptitude for running; I have to face it. But you do." He was nibbling an ear of corn that Hooyo had cooked the night before.

"And that's why you've decided to be my coach?"

"Every athlete has a coach. If I can't be an athlete, then I want to be a coach."

"So if I win I'll owe it all to you. . . ." I teased.

"No," he replied seriously, "it's because you need someone to train you. You can't do it alone." A pause. I raised my head and looked at him.

"Can't do *what*?" I asked.

"You can't become a champion."

We were eight years old.

As usual, I didn't answer him. But from that day on I had a coach.

I might have lost a playmate on account of Ahmed, though I didn't want to admit it. But I had found myself.

After that day I turned into what I had always wanted to be: an athlete.

All thanks to Alì, without his even realizing it.

I hugged him tightly and we went out to run in the wind on that afternoon of boundless joy.

CHAPTER 5

※

THEN, on a morning like any other, which gave no sign of what was about to happen, while Hodan and I were still asleep, Aabe went out as usual with Yassin to go to work in the Xamar Weyne district.

The area was a distance away but very busy, full of people coming and going, an ideal place to do business. Hundreds and hundreds of vendors hawked their products to passersby from large and small stalls in every color of the rainbow. This was the Xamar Weyne market, a raucous madhouse where the sellers were almost as numerous as the buyers. Cotton, linen, sweaters, charcoal, American jeans, shoes, fruit, sandals, vegetables, incense, spices, chocolate . . . Each one peddled his specialty.

Yassin was two years younger than Aabe and even taller, over six feet. He looked older, though: He had more wrinkles around his eyes and on his brow, and his eyes always seemed sad. Hooyo said it was because he had suffered so much over the loss of his wife, the beautiful Yasmin, Ali's mother, who had died of cancer when we were two years old. There was a framed photograph of her on a dresser in their room, and every time I went in there I was taken aback by how beautiful Yasmin was. The broad forehead, the big, elongated eyes, the same full lips that Alì had.

Every morning Aabe and Yassin left the house at five and didn't come home until around six in the evening, at sunset. They had two large stalls, Aabe's for clothes and Yassin's for vegetables.

"I hope you will never have to work as hard as I do, my little Samia," Aabe, exhausted, always told me when I was little, before saying good night to me in the evening. I loved having him there close to me: Those moments were magical for me. I would lose myself in the scent of his aftershave and I was happy; I felt safe. Even his clothes had a smell. It was the smell of Aabe's clothes after a long day's work; I would have recognized it among thousands.

"If you can do it, so can I," I told him.

"I'm doing it so that you won't have to."

"Aabe," I said once after thinking about it for a while, "how come you never complain about what you do? Omar Sheikh, our landlord, is always complaining about everything. Whenever he's here he spends all his time telling us about his hard luck."

"Complaining only makes you keep doing what you don't like," Aabe answered in his deep voice, as he ran a hand through his flowing black hair. He had always worn his hair long. Hooyo teased him, saying he acted like a woman and that's why he didn't have a beard either. "Beards are for fundamentalists," he would tell her. "If you really don't like something, you just need to change it, my little Samia. I love my work, and I love it because I do it for you. This makes me happy."

I stopped to think a little, then asked him: "Papa, aren't you ever afraid of the war?"

He turned serious. "You must never say you're afraid, my Samia. Never. Otherwise the things you're afraid of will seem big and they'll think they can beat you."

That morning he and Yassin left together, as always. They had just crossed Jamaral Daud, right beyond the parliament, and had stopped at their friend Taageere's bar, a wooden shack in a small alley, to drink a *shaat* and shoot the breeze before work, as they did every day.

Suddenly, however, they heard gunshots.

A hundred yards away, from behind a six-story building, four or five Hawiye militiamen, affiliated with us Abgal, had appeared. They were looking for a Darod who, according to them, had stolen something, and they were shouting that he must have fled in that direction.

One of them spotted Yassin standing with Aabe in front of the bar and pointed him out to the others, and they all started running toward him.

Aabe and Yassin didn't even have time to think.

When the soldiers came closer, Ali's father realized what was about to happen and instinctively started to run away.

It all happened in an instant.

As soon as Yassin turned his back, one of the men opened fire, followed immediately by the others.

Aabe lunged to knock Yassin to the ground, clear of the barrage of bullets that had already riddled the wall a few inches from there.

Later they told us that Taageere stood there the whole time as if frozen, the two glasses of *shaat* in his hands, poised in midair.

Meanwhile, the gunfire was over as quickly as it had erupted.

The soldiers shouted something and, satisfied, disappeared around the corner as swiftly as they had materialized.

Aabe and Yassin turned, relieved, thinking they had come through it safely.

But when they tried to get up, they realized what had happened. Taageere was white as a sheet.

Aabe had been shot in his right foot.

He hadn't even been aware of it.

The blood had already formed a small pool.

Friendly fire had struck an Abgal in place of a Darod.

HODAN COMPOSED HER SONGS and then sang them.

She had a beautiful voice, like velvet. It was a little husky and low but at the same time clear enough to reach the highest notes. When she sang, her smooth, round, porcelain-doll face wore an astonished expression, as if she were always about to reveal something. I adored her. I wanted to be like her, to have her beauty, her voice. Besides that, the veils never looked as good on any other girl as they did on Hodan. The bright colors, yellow, red, and orange, lit up her face like a sudden blaze in a dense forest.

To mark the rhythm she would join her palms and tap her fingers together, like a shell in the Indian Ocean that continuously opens and shuts, following a steady tempo.

She sang in the traditional *buraanbur* form, though blended with more modern music, in the style of her musical group, the Shamsudiin Band.

She composed her songs in our room, alone, or while we kids were in bed, with the *ferus* lit, waiting to fall asleep, enjoying the last laughs of the day.

At some point, every night, Hodan withdrew, pulled out her little notebook, and began writing. She wrote about all kinds of subjects, about what made her suffer and about what gave her joy.

I watched her closely, studying her smallest gestures. She and I, in fact, had always slept next to each other, ever since I was born, when she had just turned five. Our mattresses were placed at right angles along the side of the room nearest the door, just inside the entrance. And since birth I'd gotten used to falling asleep with her voice in my ears, growing slowly softer and softer, until fading off into a whisper.

Maybe that's why I always slept well and why, as everyone said, I was confident about what would happen tomorrow, thinking it would be better than today. It was because of Hodan's voice, which had accompanied me to sleep since I was born.

"I've given all my optimism to you," she'd tell me.

Unlike me, Hodan was always worried; she always had something on her mind. She found peace only in the evening, when the *ferus* was turned off and she could go on whispering her songs about the war, about our family, about the future, about running, about Alì, about our father being shot, about the children we would one day have.

We always fell asleep hand in hand, our heads touching. As I held her hand, I felt her grip gradually loosen and become more gentle. And I realized that she relaxed as she sang.

I knew I was her first audience, and it filled me with pride. I felt she gauged her songs by my smiles; though the themes varied widely, they all spoke of one thing: the importance of freedom and the power of dreams.

On the night Aabe was injured, while he was in the hospital recovering from surgery, Hodan composed a song that compared him to a great winged horse.

She sang it in the middle of the room, sitting cross-legged on my brother Abdi's mattress.

Hooyo was with us too; they hadn't let her sleep at the hospital. The beds couldn't be occupied by relatives, since sick people or those wounded by mortars or gunfire were continually coming in. Small and composed, Hooyo sat on my sister Ubah's mattress, right in front of me, her feet flat on the ground, not cross-legged like us. Head in hands, her eyes were fixed on Hodan. She was lost in thought; her gaze drifted here and there.

Ubah had lit incense, and the strong, sweet odor filled the small room. The song said that our father would continue to fly as he had done up to that day, and that, flying, he would ferry us into adulthood. That his arms were as vigorous as the wings of a huge bird and his legs as sturdy as the trunks of ancient trees.

For some reason, what I've always remembered about that night was the tears that silently filled our big brother Said's eyes as he stared impassively ahead of him.

I got up and went over on tiptoe to wipe them for him.

CHAPTER 6

※

FROM THE DAY he was wounded, it was clear that Aabe would no longer be able to go to work. He had lost the use of his foot, of which little more than a stump remained. From now on, he would have to lean on a stick to walk.

He would no longer be able to pull the cart with the clothes. His future would be the house, the courtyard.

After a lifetime spent together, day after day, Yassin would get up alone and by himself walk an hour to reach the Xamar Weyne market.

The first days were tough.

Aabe had withdrawn into a silence full of suppressed anger. Every so often, in the countless hours spent sitting in the wicker chair in the courtyard, he'd be seized with rage and would hurl his stick with all his might, as if it were a javelin. It would strike the wall and end up on the ground, too far away to reach. Until Hooyo recovered it for him.

In those awful days Aabe was always mute, mortified, and

inert. It was impossible to talk to him; he chased us away; he even chased me away, his darling little girl.

Only once did he come out with words that made Hooyo's tears flow. "I'm a useless object, incapable of moving, like a car without wheels."

Yassin was desperate. At first he did everything he could to try to help him. He'd even offered to make the trip to the market twice, once with his cart and a second time with Aabe's. Then he gave up; he saw that it would take time. A long time, an infinite time.

It took three months.

One evening, after supper, while we girls were playing *shentral*, Aabe asked Yassin to go get the cards; he wanted to play a game.

It was the first time he'd spoken to someone since it had all happened.

Yassin as usual was near the *burgico*, staring at the coals flickering and crackling.

When he heard Aabe speak, he stood up and, without saying a word, went to get the cards and table and brought them to where his friend was sitting.

They played three hands of *scopa*, a card game that the Italians had taught their fathers and that some people still knew. They played without saying a word.

Then Aabe won, or Yassin let him win (no one was ever able to say), and Aabe banged his fist on the table and said in his deep voice: "A toast! To your usual shameless good luck. I lose a foot and win at *scopa*. May a thousand liters of boiling *shaat* fall on your head."

From that day on, slowly but surely, everything went back to being the way it had always been.

Aabe and Yassin became best friends again and, with their friendship, everything else fell into place.

One evening, when Aabe had grown used to going out and being seen in the neighborhood with the cane that he still despised, Yassin came to our parents' room.

After a while we were all called in; Yassin wanted us to hear.

In a broken voice he said that he would be indebted to our family for the rest of his life and that he would like to take care of us but didn't know how he could; his resources were barely enough for his children.

Then he took an envelope from a pouch and handed it to Hooyo.

She looked at Aabe, who nodded; then she opened it. It contained money.

"It's all I have," Yassin said, "but I beg you to accept it in front of your family as a symbol of my gratitude for having saved me, brother Yusuf."

Aabe looked at him in silence with a faint smile on his lips. "Call your children in, but first dry those tears," he told him as he settled himself comfortably in the wicker chair.

When Alì and his brothers arrived, Aabe cleared his throat. "It is thanks to you, my friend," he began, "that I am still alive to realize that this war cannot be right."

Yassin's sons looked at one another.

Nassir had sat down on the ground and Alì had gone to sit between his legs; he looked up at Aabe, not understanding what was happening.

"How is it possible that my brothers can almost kill an Abgal like themselves?" Aabe went on, drawing Alì's attention. "This stump is testimony to the fact that the war cannot be right."

Then Aabe called me and Alì into the center of the room.

He ordered us to shake hands and hug each other.

We were bewildered. Alì, withdrawn as usual, didn't tear his eyes away from his bare feet.

Then he obeyed. He held out his hand without looking at me.

I shook it.

"Now promise me," Aabe continued, "that you, an Abgal, and you, a Darod, will live forever in peace. That you will never hate each other and never hate the other clans."

Hands still tightly clasped, we promised.

Then Aabe asked if we knew that war was the result of hatred that makes people blind and content only with blood.

Together we said yes.

Finally he asked: "Do you know that we are all Somali brothers, regardless of tribes and clans? Well, Samia? Alì?" he thundered like when he was angry. "Do you know that?"

"Yes," Alì said in a faint voice, still staring at the floor.

"Yes," I echoed him.

Then Aabe asked Hodan to sing us a song, there in the bedroom.

There were so many of us, packed in tightly. Fourteen people crowded in a small room with two mattresses on the floor and mud walls, talking about peace and hope while outside there was a war.

This too was Aabe.

MY MOTHER HAD already made up her mind, and in any case there weren't many alternatives.

She didn't like the idea of selling men's clothes; she said it wasn't a proper job for a woman. So, after repeated urging by Yassin, she decided that she would start selling fruits and vegetables.

At first Yassin gave her his produce to sell.

Then she gradually began to acquire it on her own, buying it in the evening from the farm workers in the area, at the same prices Yassin paid after twenty years of work.

Some weeks later, Hooyo went along with a woman friend who had a stall in another district, off limits to the Darod but even busier than Xamar Weyne: Abde Aziz.

And she became a fruits and vegetables vendor.

We lived that way for more than a year, poorer than we'd ever been, until everything changed in my life and Hodan's.

I won my first race and she got engaged to Hussein, a Darod boy from a good family who played in her band.

CHAPTER 7

❀

THE DAY I TURNED TEN was also the day of the race through the city's districts. The war was increasingly violent, and everything was becoming more difficult, even organizing the annual race, which for me was the most important thing in the world: In fact, sixteen months had passed since the previous one, rather than twelve. With the war, even the length of a year changed: Time stretched out as the violence dragged on.

Throughout that period Alì was a good coach.

He knew when to force me to go on exercising even though I'd had enough, and at the same time he understood how to motivate me.

I trained and trained during those months; I wanted to win at all costs.

To win for me. To win to prove to myself and everyone else that the war could put an end to some things but not everything. To win to make Aabe and Hooyo happy.

Aabe must have sensed my agitation because that morning he called me over to him and told me that he knew one day I would become a champion. He had never said anything like that before.

He'd been tender at times, but he had never gone so far as to encourage me.

From the pocket of his khaki pants he pulled out a white Nike headband, the kind you wear over your forehead to absorb the sweat.

It must have been left over from the clothes that he was no longer able to sell, piled up along with a thousand other odds and ends in the big room next to that of Alì and his brothers.

I hugged him tightly. His cane, leaning against the back of his wicker chair, almost fell over.

"Samia, if you win today, I promise you that the next race you run will be with a pair of new sneakers," he said, settling the band on my head as if it were a crown.

I couldn't believe my ears.

A new pair was something I had never even dreamed of owning. I was running with sneakers that no longer fit Said and that had already been worn by Abdi and Shafici. This meant that the right shoe had a hole at the toe and the left had a sole so worn that it was like running barefoot. I felt everything I stepped on: pebbles, seeds, branches, twigs, everything. And I lost my concentration, because I had to be careful to steer clear of animal bones or cans of motor oil tossed along the street and watch out for crevices or deep, gaping holes in the ground.

"I promise I'll do everything I can to deserve the shoes, Aabe," I vowed, touching the terrycloth headband with my fingers to convince myself it was real.

"Just how far do you hope to go, hmm?" he asked me, squeezing my cheeks with his big hand and wagging my face from side to side. He was joking, but I took it seriously, as always when it came to running.

"Aabe, I'm ten years old now."

"Yes, and that's another reason why if you win . . ."

I didn't let him finish. "I'm ten and you'll see, when I'm seventeen I'll run in the Olympics. That's how far I want to go."

He started laughing.

"Aabe, I'm going to run in the 2008 Olympics, when I'm seventeen. That's my goal," I repeated that morning. "You'll see." I paused. "In fact, one day I'll even win."

"So tell me . . . where will the 2008 Olympics be held, here in Somalia?" he asked wryly, knowing full well that wasn't possible.

"No. In China," I said, still fingering the headband.

"Ah, in China. So you're going to China, then?"

"Of course, I can't run in the Chinese Olympics from here, Aabe."

At that point he looked at me seriously. He'd finally realized that I wasn't joking.

"All right, Samia, I believe you," he said, stroking my hair. "If you're so determined, then you'll get there for sure."

Then he shifted in his chair as if to look at me more closely, for the first time seeing me with new eyes. "You're a little warrior running for freedom," he said. "Yes, you're a real little warrior." As he spoke he started adjusting the elastic band on my forehead. Our fingers touched. "If you really believe it, then one day you will lead Somali women to liberation from the bondage in which men have placed them. You will be their leader, my little warrior."

It was the first time I'd said that about the Olympics and also the first time it had popped into my head. I had never thought of it before. Yet as soon as I said it, nothing seemed more real to me.

Aabe's promise of a gift must have been enough to spark something inside of me that I didn't even know I had. His words had officially sealed my heart.

That day Alì took me to the start of the race in a wheelbarrow so I wouldn't get tired. I tried to get out of it every way I could, but he insisted, saying he was my coach and that I had to do whatever he ordered. And so I arrived at the start on that throne.

Alì had planned it all out: He left me there and rode a neighborhood boy's bike up to the stadium to get there early and be waiting for me at the finish line.

It was the usual seven-kilometer route that I had run a thousand times, not a short-distance speed race, which I was better at. But I was thin as a rail and weighed little more than a feather, as Alì said, so I had some advantage over the others.

"You have to learn to fly, Samia," he kept telling me. "If you learn to fly, you'll beat them all."

I was so light that if I learned to catch the wind I would easily be as fast as a rocket; that was his theory.

At first it sounded silly, but then I thought more about it. Maybe he was right. I had to try to make myself as light as possible, direct my weight upward. And try to stay on the outer edge, so I wouldn't have anyone in back of me and could let the wind push me from behind. Then, once I was out in front, it would all be easier. No one would steal my air.

What I had to do was minimize the contact my feet made with the ground.

I had to learn to fly.

That day, when the starter pistol went off, I forgot everything.

It had never happened to me before, but since then it hasn't failed to happen, every time I've won. My mind was able to create a blank and focus only on positive things.

On the day of my tenth birthday I realized that running freed me from my thoughts. And so, meter by meter, kilometer after kilometer, the skinny little girl was able to overtake the majority of the group and get behind the four fastest runners.

In my head were Aabe's words and the way he had tugged the terry headband down over my forehead.

"One day you will lead Somali women to liberation from the bondage in which men have placed them. You will be their leader, my little warrior."

From that day on, every time I raced I clocked off meter after meter mulling over those redemptive words of my father, the words of Yusuf Omar Nur, son of Omar Nur Mohamed.

The liberation of my people and of the women of Islam.

That day I won.

For the first time. My first victory.

The race ended with a lap in front of a large crowd of onlookers.

The CONS stadium, used for all sporting events, was old, hammered by bullets, its rickety stands shored up with planks to reduce the risk of collapse, the track riddled with shrapnel from grenades.

Since the start of the war, the new stadium has been used as a depository for the army. Instead of athletes, there were tanks and soldiers on the field. Officers rather than spectators in the stands.

From a distance, as I neared the old stadium, exhausted, I realized how decrepit it was, mutilated by bombs.

At five hundred meters from that ruined structure I was still in fourth place.

When I turned onto Jidka Warshaddaha, with the stadium's irregular shape on the horizon, I heard Alì's voice in my head urging me to put the wind at my back and go on to win.

I don't know where I got the strength, but I began to fly. I passed the two guys in front of me, one after the other.

At the entrance to the stadium my legs nearly started shaking when I saw the multitude of people sitting in the stands. You could feel their excitement, their expectations, the fact that they were there to see someone win.

And I wanted to be that someone.

I entered the stadium second. Meter by meter on the pitted tartan track, I realized that the runner in first place had not measured out his energies well. I felt I still had some in reserve, while he was plodding along, worn out, losing ground with every step.

Then the miracle happened: The people in the stands began yelling and calling me *abaayo*. Sister.

They'd seen that I was faster and they wanted me to win.

They were cheering me on: *abaayo, abaayo*.

Every word gave me an extra boost.

After the first curve I had already caught up to the front runner, and in four strides I passed him.

At that point the fans rose to their feet, incredulous and excited. They were all applauding the little *abaayo*.

A rhythmic applause spurred me on.

Clap-clap. Clap-clap. Clap-clap.

My legs flowed ahead like waves driven by an energy that wasn't mine; the spectators were the ones pulling me along, like a tractor towing a trailer or like the gravitational pull of the moon and the sun on the sea's tides.

I crossed the finish line first.

It seemed unbelievable to me.

I ran the last few meters after the finish with arms raised, carried along by the rush of all those kilometers.

Then I bent over my legs and felt a strange warmth on my cheeks: unwanted tears on the little warrior's face.

I quickly wiped them away before standing up, dead tired but brimming with energy. I could have turned around and retraced the entire course, from start to finish.

Around me the crowd was cheering and shouting, jubilant and ecstatic.

As they went wild with applause, I could read their thoughts: *It's incredible that she won, she's little more than a child.*

It was incredible to me too.

But after a few stunned minutes, a medal was slipped around my neck.

Which told me that it was all true.

Alì and I waited in the locker room for the crowd to leave the stadium. He talked to a lot of people who asked him who I was.

He introduced himself as my coach, and it made everyone laugh, because he was only ten years old. He was tall for his age, tall and skinny, but he too was little more than a child. Yet for years he'd been acting like a grown man.

To get home we retraced the route of the race.

Alì told me how he'd felt when he saw me enter the gate of the stadium and how excited the crowd had been when I passed the other runners. He was all keyed up.

Now and then, as often happened, we'd run into someone who would look me up and down and, seeing me dressed as a boy, would shake his head or mutter a few words under his breath before moving on.

About halfway home we were stopped by an old man with a long beard and bony face.

After looking at me disapprovingly, he started in with the same old story. "Where are the *qamar*, the *hijab*, and the *diric*, huh, girlie? Did you perhaps forget to get dressed today?"

"She's an athlete, sir," Alì answered for me. "And she just won a race. She commands the respect that athletes deserve."

It was the first time I heard it said publicly that I was an athlete.

The old man looked at us and rolled his eyes, not knowing what to say. "And you? If she's an athlete, who might you be?" he asked.

"I'm her coach. And her spokesman. When this athlete becomes known throughout the world someday, you, sir, will remember this conversation."

At that point we looked at each other and burst out laughing.

The man muttered something and walked away, shaking his head.

I had become an athlete. For the second time, from the day Alì decided that he would be my coach. But this time it was more real.

By now it was late afternoon and the wind had suddenly risen, and when the wind starts blowing, there are only two things you can do in Mogadishu: keep your mouth shut to prevent the dust from drying out your throat for the rest of your days and quickly look for shelter somewhere so you won't get coated from head to toe.

We filled our lungs and started running home.

I wasn't tired at all. I could have run for another ten hours straight.

All of a sudden, at the intersection with the big avenue, a copy of the newspaper *Banadir* plunged down from the sky like a dive-bombing meteorite, carried from somewhere by the wind.

It hit me right on the shoulder, then fell to the ground, open to a full-size photo of a young man who immediately looked familiar.

Curious, I bent to grab the paper before it flew away again.

It was the face of Mo Farah, the runner who'd left Mogadishu when he was more or less my age to seek refuge in England; there a proficient coach was leading him to win numerous major races.

He had always been one of my heroes, someone to look up to. Born in Somalia like me, he had gone on to run and win throughout the world.

News of his victories and his talent often reached us.

Whenever I listened to something about him on the radio at Taageere's bar or heard someone mention his name, I felt my stomach clench, due partly to anger, because he had managed to get away, and partly to never-ending admiration, so boundless it made me dream of becoming like him.

The headline said that Mo was a champion and that Somalia had made him flee.

Alì was already far ahead of me; he had continued running. I snatched the page hastily, folded it, and followed Alì home.

As I ran I thought that Mo's face, which had looked at me in the wind, must be a sign.

A medal in one hand and a folded sheet of newspaper in the other, I let myself be carried along, transported lightly by the squally gusts.

When we got home, Alì told everybody about my victory before making the rounds to display the trophy.

Hooyo was moved, and Hodan and Hamdi teased her, imitating her wiping away her tears with a handkerchief and then blowing her nose with a big spluttering honk.

Nassir and Ahmed were also there, in a corner near the wall, sitting on the ground playing *griir*. Ahmed. It had been a while since I'd seen him; he didn't come to the courtyard so often anymore.

When Alì got to them with the medal in his hand, Ahmed didn't even raise his head from the pebbles. Nassir glanced at his little brother and then went back to talking to his friend.

Alì stood there frozen. Both Ahmed's and Nassir's eyes looked cruel, hostile, the pupils dilated.

Yassin had been watching the whole scene from the table where he was playing cards with Aabe. "Pay attention to your brother, Nassir," his father shouted to him from there.

Nassir and Ahmed gave no sign that they were even present.

They went on with their slow, mechanical gestures, as if the world around them didn't exist, as if we were all mere shadows in their minds.

"Nassir! I told you not to ignore Alì!" Yassin shouted louder, rising menacingly from his chair.

Nassir looked up in slow motion and said, in a deliberate monotone: "I saw, Aabe, I saw it. Calm down. It's Samia's medal. The one she won today. I saw it. Sorry, but it doesn't interest me much. Don't get riled up over such a little thing. Go back to your card game."

Yassin stared at him bitterly, then looked disheartened. He mumbled something under his breath about Ahmed and waved a hand as if to say, *The hell with him*. Then he sat down again.

From where I was I heard him confide to Aabe: "I can't do it alone. Without my Yasmin, every now and then I feel like I just can't do it."

"Don't be silly," Aabe told him. "You just have to forbid Nassir from seeing that friend of his."

Then Aabe called Alì, who had been standing stock still in the middle of the courtyard.

Without saying a word, Alì came over with his head down, the medal still clutched in his hand. He seemed very little. A little child. Which, in fact, he was.

Aabe and Yassin tried to tell him something to make him smile, but by now it was no use. His good mood had vanished in an instant. Seeing Ahmed was all it took.

Then Aabe clapped his hands and everyone sang a traditional hymn to my victory.

After that day, Ahmed never again showed up at our house.

That evening, after supper, there was a big party for me. Hussein, Hodan's fiancé, who had been sitting beside her and Hooyo all evening, had brought a sesame cake that his mother had made for the occasion. If I'd won, the cake would be to celebrate; if not, to console me.

Hussein and Hodan were now talking about marriage; our two families had already met, and his family had indicated that he would soon ask for Hodan's hand.

Aabe hadn't had to think twice.

He liked the young man, who was already twenty, five years older than Hodan, and he also liked Hussein's father, his daughter's future father-in-law. A family more well off than ours. He was happy to give his consent.

Soon Hodan and Hussein would marry.

When I heard that, I got jealous; I didn't want anyone to take my favorite sister away. But then I tried to understand. I saw that Hodan was happy, and I was happy for her.

Besides, Hussein was pleasant, polite, and always well dressed; he liked me right away and called me "champion."

That night everyone was happy for me, but the happiest of all was Aabe, who took me aside, kissed me on the head, and whispered in my ear: "Good for you, my little one. I told you you could do it."

Then he got up, with the help of his ever-present cane, and limped to his room. When he came back he was holding a large black plastic bag. Inside was a pair of sneakers. White. Brand new, like none I'd ever seen before.

I could have swooned with joy.

I put them on and started leaping up and down like an idiot.

Then I looked around for Alì, my coach.

He wasn't there.

Yassin shook his head and nodded to their room.

Alì had withdrawn. Again. Ahmed's presence had that effect on him.

At least this time he hadn't retreated to the eucalyptus.

I approached soundlessly, and after a while I popped in, showing off the shoes.

Alì lay on his mattress on his stomach, his face hidden in the crook of his arm. I tried to talk to him, but he didn't answer me. I asked him if he wanted to try on the shoes, and again it was as if he hadn't heard me.

If he hadn't reacted to that, nothing would budge him. A pair of brand-new sneakers would normally have revived him.

It was all Ahmed's fault.

I wanted to make Ahmed pay, even though he was good-looking enough to take my breath away. But it was my party. I was an athlete and I had won that day: Now I should just celebrate.

After two hours of dancing around and singing, I couldn't wait to go to bed and tell Hodan about the sheet of newspaper that I had hidden under the mattress.

That afternoon, in fact, I had come home with a medal, but also with a challenge: One day I would win the Olympics and Hodan would become a famous singer, thanks in part to her husband's family, and would compose our people's hymn of liberation.

But unlike Mo Farah, we would both do it without leaving Somalia.

I would win wearing the blue jersey with the white star. And the same for her. We would show the way for the liberation of women and then lead our country out of war.

I was sure of it: In my heart I felt that together we had the power to change our world.

That night, in bed, I talked to her about these things.

Hodan held my hand tightly and said yes.

We would never leave Mogadishu. We would not flee. We would become the symbol of liberation. Before falling asleep I slipped the medal under the mattress and took out the page with Mo Farah's face. I wet the four corners of the sheet with a little saliva and stuck it on the mud wall a few inches from my head.

Looking into his eyes, in silence, I made a promise to Mo Farah as well. I would become a champion like him. But he, every night, would have to remind me.

CHAPTER 8

❀

A FEW MONTHS LATER, a few weeks after her sixteenth birthday, Hodan got married.

The *aroos*, the wedding celebration, was unforgettable. It was held in a splendid, elegantly decorated hall that Hussein's family had rented, as was traditional. There were hours and hours of food, talk, and dancing with half the people in our neighborhood, which was the same one in which Hussein lived.

Hodan was wearing a white dress that had been our mother's, and she was stunning, radiant. I had never seen her so beautiful.

The previous night I hadn't slept. Not even a wink. We held each other's hands the whole time, and when she finally fell asleep, I kept thinking that this would be the last time we'd lie so close at night. In the morning when I woke up, my eyes were swollen from crying and rimmed with dark circles.

Still, the seven days of festivities were wonderful. I had never seen anything more spectacular in my life.

We girls and Hooyo were very vibrant in our *qamar*, *diric*, and *garbasar* in every color of the rainbow. Veils, veils, veils. And how light and fluttery and magical all those veils were! I've never liked covering up my hair and body but that day, for the first time, I felt pride in wearing traditional garments.

Not that morning, though, when I was embarrassed to leave the room with everyone waiting in the courtyard to see me as they never had before.

I didn't want to come out. There were no mirrors in the room, but even without seeing myself, I felt uncomfortable.

I was sitting on the edge of the mattress, all dressed up, when Hooyo came in.

As soon as she saw me, her lips widened in a broad smile. "You're beautiful, my daughter. Come on, stand up."

"I feel ridiculous, Hooyo. I don't want to be seen like this," I said softly as I got up.

Without saying a word she went out and came back with a white veil and a large mirror that she had borrowed from a neighbor. She arranged the white veil around my shoulders and then, with a clip, gathered my hair into a twist at the back of my head. She used a pencil to outline my eyes and applied red lipstick to my mouth. I stood motionless the whole time, like a stone statue.

Hooyo took a few steps back and repeated: "You look beautiful, my daughter. If it weren't your sister getting married, I would say that today you look more beautiful than the bride."

Then she picked up the mirror that she'd leaned against the wall and told me to look at myself.

I was stunned by what I saw. In the glass there was no longer a little child but a young girl with even, delicate features, beautiful.

It was me, and I was beautiful. I would never have believed it.

As soon as I stepped shyly out the door, Hodan gave me a look of pure admiration. "You're beautiful, my little *abaayo*," she said, moved, as Hooyo hastened to wipe away the tears that threatened to cause her makeup to run.

"It's you who are beautiful, my dear young bride Hodan," I replied, using words that are customary on a wedding day. "Don't forget us."

We celebrated feverishly for hours. Even Aabe danced with all of us daughters, supported by his buddy, the cane.

Then he and Hooyo danced in each other's arms in a way that no one had ever seen; they looked like an engaged couple deeply in love. Hooyo was radiant in her white veils: In a single day she'd shed twenty years, as if she were our sister.

We carried on like that, singing and dancing, late into the night, to live *niiko* music played by the Shamsudiin Band. But the most moving part of the whole *aroos* was Hodan's singing. As a surprise, she had written a song for each of the people she held dear. One for Hooyo, full of gentleness and gratitude; one for Aabe, full of hope and promise; one for Hussein, overflowing with pure love; and one for me, her little warrior sister. At the table we pulled out our handkerchiefs and cried like babies until she'd finished. It was a low blow, unfair; we'd make her pay.

Everyone, however, was awaiting the most entertaining moment of the wedding: testing Hussein. It's a tradition that serves to show the bride's family that the groom will be able to cope with any eventuality.

The most enthusiastic challenger was an uncle of Hussein's, a very funny man, short and bald, with a long, thin mustache.

Poor Hussein had less than five minutes to obtain a basket of fresh fruit for the bride.

Outside the hall was a large field planted with watermelons. Hussein came back with a single huge watermelon. It weighed so much that his arms nearly gave out, his smile slipped, and his legs faltered.

Then he had to wring a chicken's neck. We all went out into the garden to wait for Hussein to get up the courage to do something he'd never dared do before. His relatives explained that the hen was very old, and wringing its neck would only be doing it a favor. Hussein took off his jacket and rolled up the sleeves of his starched shirt while the poor creature squawked and flapped around awkwardly. I kept my eyes closed the whole time, and the hen's terrified screeches gave me goose bumps. I opened my eyes again only when I heard the final applause.

As a final test, Hussein had to prove that he was strong enough to carry Hodan to the table where Aabe and Hooyo were sitting; it was to the right of the bride and groom's table, along an obstacle course that his cousins had set up while he was busy with the chicken. It was the last straw and Hodan, merciless, laughed and laughed.

Everything had been perfect; we were elated.

The closer we came to the end of the weeklong celebration of the *aroos*, however, the more I felt a pall of sadness come over me.

After tomorrow my beloved sister would no longer be with me; she would go to live in Hussein's parents' house. It would no longer be me she'd sing to sleep but Hussein. No longer would she hold my hand tightly; no longer would she lead me to the most wonderful dreams of hope and liberation.

She would do all these things with him.

I would have to settle for mornings.

Every day, in fact, Hodan and I continued to see each other to go to school. We met halfway between her new home and ours, which were barely half a kilometer apart, and we walked the last stretch together.

She described what it was like to be a wife at sixteen and live in the home of people who loved you but who, in the end, were strangers. She told me that you had no choice but to grow up. It made me think that I certainly didn't want to get married; each day I was more and more convinced that the only things I really wanted to be wed to were a tartan track with no holes and a good pair of running shoes with cleats. Every morning when we met, Hodan hugged me, kissed the top of my head, and told me she missed me. I admitted that since she'd gone I occasionally had bad dreams. Then she asked about everyone, about Aabe and Hooyo, about our brothers and sisters; she wanted to be filled in on every detail, even though she and Hussein came to our house for supper at least once a week.

She needed to know everything, as if we were light-years away. Her eyes flashed with impatience and nostalgia until I described every single minute of our new home life.

The school we went to wasn't large or even attractive: The walls were peeling and the desks were worn; still, it was a school, and I liked it there. I enjoyed the classes, especially gym, where I was the best, but also arithmetic and accounting. My favorite thing of all, though, was the geometry theorems. It was amazing to learn that there were laws hidden in the world around us: in the rectangles of courtyards or in outhouse pits. Or, for example, in the circle that the *burgico* left on the ground after cooking. It seemed magical, and it gave me a sense of assurance. If there were rules that explained it, the universe couldn't be so bad. Maybe someday we would come to discover the laws that led men to wage war, and when that day came we would eliminate it forever. It would be the greatest day in the history of mankind.

But the best part of school took place during recess. Hodan and I had always eaten rice and vegetables, which were never lacking, especially once Hooyo had started working. But now, since Hodan lived in a household that was more prosperous than ours, she would sometimes bring meat. Hussein, like his father, was an electrician, and in a country at war, given everything that ends up ruined or destroyed each day, there's never any lack of work for an electrician.

I ate in five minutes and spent the rest of the time playing. Hide and seek, for instance. There weren't many places to hide, so you had to use your wits. Sometimes I sat down on the ground with a group of girls who were eating or talking in the yard, hoping to go unnoticed. Or I'd duck behind the trunk of an acacia. Or behind the big trash bin. Or behind the teachers, who laughed when we crouched under their *garbasar,* shawls. Anyway, even when they discovered me, I was always the fastest to reach the back wall of the courtyard.

In the afternoon Hodan and I returned home knowing that we had spent the day usefully. Aabe always told us: *"Mangiate la ʒuppa finché è calda.* Eat the soup while it's hot!" Another one of his Italian proverbs. Try to take pleasure in school. Think of it as a privilege, not as something boring. Enjoy it while the money lasts, because with the war we live from day to day.

When it was time for Hodan and me to part, at the corner of avenue Jamaral Daud, there were tears. Hers and mine, every day.

It didn't matter that we would see each other the next morning: We didn't want to be separated. In fact, we made up a thousand excuses to stay together.

Once in a while I went to hear her sing with the Shamsudiin Band. There were about a dozen musicians who met three afternoons a week in a large concert hall, or what was left of it, in the area of the old port, near the sea.

To get there you had to turn onto a street from which, for a stretch, you could see the shore on the horizon between the houses.

Sometimes we did everything we could not to look in that direction. But there were days when it was too painful, days when the sun shone brightly in a blue sky and a fresh wind blew in from offshore. It was especially hard for Hodan, who had gone swimming and played in the sand as a child, and remembered how exquisite it was.

On those days, if we were happy or carefree, one of us would simply say: "Should we look at it?"

The other always answered yes. Then we would duck into a space between the houses so we wouldn't risk bumping into some militiamen, and we'd stay there gazing at the sea for an hour. We never even thought about venturing out onto the sand, as I used to do with Alì when I was little.

We squatted there in a narrow gap between two houses, staring at the horizon, and didn't breathe a word, our *garbasar* trailing in the fine white dust.

The sun's play on the waves made our thoughts soar. There was no need for words. At those moments everything was exactly as it should be; we didn't ask for anything more, for anything to change. Just to be together forever like that.

Going to hear Hodan sing was fabulous. Behind the platform where the group played hung a well-known Somali proverb—or maybe it was well known only to me, because Hodan was always repeating it to me: *Durbaab garabkaga ha kugu jiro ama gacalgaaga ha kuu rumo*, which means "Let the music play; all we need is music." It was her motto and her reason for being.

Hodan sat on a chair in the center of the group, marking the rhythm by tapping her fingers, palms joined; every so often she clapped her palms in a *sacab*, a stronger beat that served to mark a pause for the other members. Behind her were the players of the *shareero*, a kind of lyre, and the *kaban*, a lute, then all the others with drums and the *shambal*, two pieces of wood with a hole in the middle; beside her was someone who played the *gobeys*, a somewhat strange flute. There was also someone playing the *koor*, the bell that a camel wears around its neck; at first this made me laugh, because it seemed like such a simple instrument that even a camel could play it—there was no need for a man.

When she was able to sing her songs, Hodan was transformed.

Her face relaxed. As soon as she started a tune, she let the music of her own voice carry her away, closing her eyes and smiling with an ecstatic expression.

When I told her that on the way home, she got embarrassed. "You look like you're in ecstasy when you sing. Like you're having an orgasm," I said, just to make her blush.

"Don't be silly. You don't even know what you're talking

about," she replied, turning her face away because she knew she'd turned red.

"Of course I do. Alì tells me all about what it's like to have sex! His friend Nurud says he already did it once and that women make funny faces when they're in ecstasy, as if they were praying to Allah and Allah suddenly answered their prayer."

"Well, tell Alì that his friend doesn't know anything about it."

"They're the same faces you make when you sing!"

"I don't make faces when I sing!" Hodan got angry and said that from then on she would sing with her back to the audience or with a paper bag over her head.

The rehearsals usually went on for two or three hours, and after a while I got bored. At that point I'd go to the back of the room and do some stretches, since at that time Alì was insisting that I develop the muscles of my legs, which to me, skinny as I was, always seemed to be stretched to the breaking point.

CHAPTER 9

❀

SINCE HODAN HAD GONE, almost every night Alì came
and played with me on the empty mattress.

. Often he ended up falling asleep, then waking up suddenly
and crossing the courtyard to go back to sleep in the room he
shared with his father and brothers.

At first he consoled me over Hodan's absence.

As soon as we finished eating, rather than stay outside in the
courtyard and play as we had always done, we went into the bedroom and, in the moonlight, with the *ferus* turned off, we talked
until my brothers and sisters came in. We talked mainly about
the future, as we had when we were little and used to spend our
afternoons in the eucalyptus tree. But we were older now, I could
tell by Alì's hands, which seemed huge to me. Alì saw me as a
champion hailed around the world; he said that someday people
from all corners of the globe would travel kilometers just to meet
me, to have their picture taken with me and shake my hand. I

laughed and couldn't imagine such a thing. I said that if that were so, I would feel guilty: Traveling all that way just to meet me didn't make sense. Then he grabbed my hand with those long, bony fingers of his, shook it, and said: "Can you picture all those people who'll want to shake your hand, like I'm doing now?"

He, however, was not going to stay in Somalia. He told me he was going to do what Mo Farah had done. As soon as he was a little bigger, because you couldn't make the Journey, as everyone called it, when you were eleven. It was too dangerous. He would go all the way to the uppermost part of Europe; for sure he wouldn't stop at Italy or Greece.

Like Mo, he would go straight to England.

As he spoke, he stared at the photograph on the wall with a faraway look. A friend of his brother's who had made the Journey had told him that in the countries of northern Europe, if you were a refugee fleeing from war they gave you a house and a stipend. But for Alì England was still the land of opportunity and besides, he said, it wasn't as cold as in Finland or Sweden, where you could freeze to death when you went out shopping.

We always said the same things. Talking about our future reassured us; it made us feel good. Not just because we could occasionally hear the firing of nearby mortars from outside. No, it was just talking about it that mattered.

Alì loved to talk, and I loved listening to him. We loved the way the story had evolved since the first time it had come out of his mouth, the way it had settled on the things that he or I liked best. It was reassuring to know how it would end; it was a nice way to spend our evenings. Not quite like Hodan's sweet voice, but almost. During those weeks, those months, Alì and I shared everything we had, generous and unafraid: We exchanged dreams.

And then there were times when we fought, when he said that someday, as a champion, I would want to leave my country. He could say anything, but not that. I knew that someday things would change, and I was sure that I would play an important role in that change. But Alì said that in the end I would give in, that I too would go to England and, like Mo Farah, I would run wearing the jersey of the country ruled by the queen. With that jersey I would win the Olympics.

He did it to infuriate me, and he succeeded. When he said that I would marry Mo and that we would be the most famous sports couple in the world, I tried not to lose my temper, but I couldn't help it. I slapped him. He laughed and slapped me back. Then he pushed me on my back on the mattress, grabbed both of my arms, climbed astride me, pinned my wrists under his knees, and tickled me until I begged for mercy with tears in my eyes, imploring him to stop.

"Only if you admit that someday you'll leave Somalia and marry Mo Farah," he said as he continued tickling me to death.

"No!" I yelled.

"Then I won't stop!"

At that point I couldn't take it anymore and I gave in. "Okay, okay, all right, you win. . . . I'll leave the country . . ."

"You'll leave the country and . . . ?"

"I'll leave the country and . . . I'll marry Mo Farah," I gasped.

"You see? I was right!"

Then we burst out laughing and made up. Every now and then one of the adults, hearing our screams, stuck his head inside.

Seeing us play, he said something we didn't even hear and quietly went back to where he'd come from.

As we lay side by side, Alì sometimes began singing. I had told him that I liked it when Hodan sang, and to tease me he started wailing in falsetto, his voice pitched artificially high like a girl's. But he was so out of tune that most times we started hitting each other and tickling again.

When we were together, Alì went back to being the way he'd always been. Only when he was with me did the melancholy that now always clouded his eyes fade.

I was worried about him.

I had tried many times to ask him what was wrong. I'd tried to talk about Ahmed, who hadn't been seen at our house since the night I'd won the annual race; I reminded him of the encounter that long-ago evening when Ahmed had protected us from the two fundamentalist kids. But Alì never responded.

Just raising the subject made him darken even more. So he won and we didn't talk about it.

We never talked about it, for two whole years.

CHAPTER 10

✤

BY DAY, HOWEVER, every day for two years Alì continued to be my coach. He had gone to the city's old library and borrowed all the training manuals he could find. For months, every afternoon in the courtyard he forced me to read them to him. As a result, we also succeeded where we had failed a long time ago: Thanks to his passion for racing and training, Alì learned to read.

He always said that whereas the heart was the engine and breath the gasoline, the muscles were the pistons, and they had to be strong, resilient, and responsive.

In the courtyard in the afternoon or late at night, when the others were already in their rooms, he made me do reps, thirty-meter sprints, from one side to the other at maximum speed. As many as a hundred in a row. I started from the back wall and sprinted to the entrance wall. Then I turned around and did the same thing in reverse. Again and again, until I collapsed on the ground, utterly spent.

"Enough, please," I begged him, exhausted, drenched with sweat.

"Samia, do you remember the first rule? Don't complain and do everything I tell you," Alì said, sitting in the shadows on the wicker chair Aabe used in the evening. I hated him.

"No. I said enough. I'm ready to drop." I tried to move him to pity by throwing myself on the ground and pretending I was about to pass out.

At that point Alì made me get up, with the dust stuck all over me, and do another ten reps. Finally, a lap all around to cool down.

To strengthen my arm muscles, he'd made weights out of tin cans or plastic bottles he'd found in the street or at the Bakara market by filling them with sand. He liked going to the market; he loved being in crowded places with thousands of people all talking at the same time and scurrying around, jostling and shoving, bumping into one another like busy ants. I, on the other hand, didn't like it at all. Not just because of the crowds, which I hated, and the reek of sweaty armpits that collected under the blue plastic awnings hung over the stalls to protect them from the scorching sun, but also because Bakara scared me. Not only was it the biggest market, but it was also the area of the city where most terrorist attacks occurred. Killers from the clans, as well as Al-Shabaab extremists, liked having all those people together.

I never wanted to go, whereas Alì, who wasn't afraid of anything, found a thousand excuses to go back there.

As a result, he'd come up with the idea of the weights.

There were thirty-three-centiliter cans of Coca-Cola, half-liter bottles, one-and-a-half-liter bottles, and two-liter ones. All filled with sand from the beach.

For my legs he'd instead used four pieces of wood to build a kind of small scaffold on which he hung different weights, depending on the exercise I had to perform. He made me sit on a chair and put that contraption on my thigh, asking me to lift it. Or, with me standing, he placed it on my ankle, which I had to raise to my thigh. The weights were very heavy. My scrawny little legs had to make a tremendous effort. We went on like that until I begged for mercy and he, moved to compassion, let me stop.

That we did all this when we were thirteen years old seems incredible. Yet that's what we did.

In spite of this, even though we were so close, on one of the worst days of my life I betrayed Alì.

I did it out of fear, but I still betrayed him.

That day Alì hadn't kept time for me, because he'd had to go help his father at work. His brother Nassir, who usually went with Aabe Yassin, wasn't around that day.

I stealthily slipped out and ran a little lap around the block. I was on my way back home, in a narrow street with three abandoned houses, when—right about halfway—I spotted a guy with his back against the wall, staring at the ground.

He wore dark glasses and one of those black shirts the extremists wear, but he was unarmed: no machine gun, no rifle.

I tried to act like it was nothing.

When I passed him, he called to me in a soft, almost alluring voice. Maybe I was tired of running, but that's how that voice sounded to me.

"Samia."

I turned around and looked at him. I didn't know him.

How did he know my name? I turned around again and kept going.

"Samia, stop! Don't worry, I'm a friend."

Never trust anyone: Aabe had taught us that the very day we were born. I tried to continue, but the guy spoke again.

"Stop. I just need to ask you something."

He was tall and thin, with broad shoulders. Dark skin. A mass of tangled black hair and the fundamentalists' long beard covering his face.

He moved away from the wall and took a step toward me.

"Where's your friend?" Now the tone was sharp, peremptory.

"What friend?" I asked, trying to keep my voice from shaking.

"The one who's always with you, day and night."

I was scared. He'd picked that time and place because he knew that at that hour it was unlikely that anyone would come by; those who worked were at work, and the alley was deserted.

"I don't have a friend. I'm always with my sister," I replied after a slight hesitation.

"Don't pull my leg. I know very well that Alì is your friend. I know everything. I just want to know where he is," he said in a harsh voice as he moved toward me.

"I don't know. . . ."

"You're an athlete, Samia, right? You like running, don't you?" His tone had turned threatening. He was just a few steps away now. Up close he was even taller than he'd seemed before, his shoulders even broader and more powerful. The sun reflected off the dark glasses in two luminous points.

"Yes, I'm an athlete," I replied in a trembling voice.

The guy stuck his right hand behind his back, under his belt, and suddenly pulled out a long knife.

I took a step back, ending up with my heels against the wall behind me. I glanced around but saw nobody; the doorways of the houses were deserted.

He reached out his arm, pointing the blade at my left leg, then came even closer. He was way too big for me to be able to do anything.

I was petrified. Even if I'd wanted to move, my limbs did not respond to my commands.

"And an athlete needs both legs to run, right?"

I was shaking, terrified; I didn't know what to say. "Yes, both of them . . ." I stammered.

"So if you don't want to lose one, tell me where Alì is. Don't worry, I won't hurt him. I just want to talk to him. I want to know where he is and have a little chat with him."

"But I don't know where Alì is."

"And I think you do know." He took another step forward until he was right in front of me. "Well . . . ?" The blade of the knife was now in contact with my skin; I felt it red hot on my knee, sharp.

"I don't know where Alì is. . . ."

He pressed slightly and the blade scratched my skin; immediately a line of blood welled up above the kneecap. His other hand squeezed below my neck, pinning me against the wall, his face just inches from mine. I smelled the scent of his cologne and I saw my distorted face reflected in his lenses.

"You don't know. . . ." He kept increasing the pressure. "Then again, do you know what a blade does when it sinks deep into the flesh? First it cuts the tendon, then the muscle, and finally the bone."

At that moment he jerked the blade away and with the same hand, not letting go of the knife, pulled off his glasses and placed them on his head.

I recognized him then. His bloodshot, dilated eyes, so close to mine. Green as emeralds. It had been three years since I'd seen him, and he had become a man. By now he must be twenty.

Ahmed. Him again; fate was playing nasty tricks on me. Just as on that night so many years ago when he had caught me and Alì by surprise, he'd reappeared out of nowhere, threatening to cut my leg.

The shadow that for all those years had lain between me and Alì, dimming my best friend's smile, was now in front of me, transformed into flesh and blood.

Then he lowered the blade and pressed it against my leg again. I felt a sharp pain, and I was scared.

I tried as hard as I could to stop myself, but I burst into tears. Abruptly, like a fountain.

I didn't want to lose my leg; with all my heart I didn't want to. I would never in my life run again. It would be the end of my dreams, the end of my liberation, the end of everything.

"All you have to do is tell me where Alì is. . . ."

"Ahmed . . ." I faltered.

"Come on, Samia, tell me. . . ." He went on holding the blade pressed against my leg, keeping my neck clenched with his other hand, making it hard to breathe. I started coughing, but my throat was squeezed shut. Mucus started running from my nose. I was choking, and my leg felt like it was on fire.

"Go on, you can tell me . . . unless you want to say good-bye to your knee." He thrust very hard and the blade sank a couple of millimeters into the flesh. I felt faint from the pain; it was as if someone had shoved a burning ember into the pit of my stomach. I just wanted it all to end. "Come on, Samia. . . ."

He was an inch away from my face; I stared at him, eyes wide open, not breathing.

"You've turned into a really pretty girl, Samia, you know that?" he whispered in a hateful voice as he drove a knee between my legs.

I immediately pictured what was going through his head.

I gave in.

"At the market . . ." It slipped out almost against my will.

Ahmed bared his teeth in a nasty leer. "At the market *where*? Which market? Bakara?"

"At the market with Yassin . . . his father . . . at Xamar Weyne . . ."

"Good girl, Samia. Good girl. I remembered that you were a smart girl. Smart and beautiful."

Then, suddenly, he let go of me, and I collapsed on the ground like a sack of beans.

Just like that, Ahmed took off in a jiffy without saying another word.

I got up, still dazed, and ran straight home.

Without saying anything to anyone, I rinsed the scratch and sat on the ground against the wall of Ali's room, waiting, praying that he would appear in the courtyard as soon as possible with his father, Yassin. That everything was normal, that what had happened to me was just a figment of my imagination.

But it wasn't; it was all real.

I was crushed by what I had done.

If Hooyo tried to say something to me, I didn't even hear her. I was terrified at the thought of having betrayed my best friend. I felt like a bad person, someone I didn't know. I felt like I was capable of betraying my own mother, or even Hodan or Aabe. Like I was capable of betraying anyone. Including myself.

Finally, around six, Alì and his father showed up. The weight that was overwhelming me evaporated. Right away I searched for some sign in Alì's eyes. But there was nothing except the usual veil of sadness and detachment.

As soon as he arrived, he went straight to his room, head bowed. He passed me with barely a hello.

I followed him and explained what had happened: I told him he was in danger, I warned him about Ahmed, I showed him the cut on my thigh.

He wasn't surprised.

Instead he replied with something that I hadn't expected: "Nassir has left our house. My brother has moved away."

I was dumbfounded. "What do you mean, he left your house? What does that mean?"

"Last night, after supper, he admitted to Aabe that he has joined Al-Shabaab. He's been spending time with them for years. That much we knew. But yesterday he said that he wants to go to the Koranic school, to be an active member of the organization. He's decided to follow Ahmed."

I remained silent while Alì sobbed. When he stopped crying, he told me not to worry, that Ahmed wouldn't do anything to him, that Nassir would protect him.

There was a strange light in Alì's eyes as he spoke, however. As if he were elated, inspired. A light that I had never seen before, that scared me.

We fell silent; then he asked me if I could leave him alone for a while.

I left the room and went to Hooyo, who was in the courtyard starting to set up the *burgico* for supper. I tried to act like nothing was wrong, asking my mother if I could help her, but my motions were as clumsy as an elephant's.

After a while Alì came out and climbed the eucalyptus with those precise, soundless, velvety movements that made him look like a cat or a monkey. He knew that tree by heart; he knew exactly where to place his bare toes without even looking.

In no time he was at the top.

The place where no one could reach him. His place. Maybe the only one. He would come down when he got over it.

Even though Alì told me not to worry, I was miserable. I had betrayed my best friend, and that feeling stung more than the blade. That night, watching Alì swiftly scale the tree with those fluid, perfect movements of his, I felt even more alone than I had when confronted by Ahmed, who had wanted to cut my leg.

I stayed down there, leaning against the wall of his room for a while, waiting for him. Then I went to bed, my head under a very dark cloud.

CHAPTER 11

※

AFTER A FEW DAYS everything was back to normal, and as usual Alì and I avoided talking about what had happened. Things fell into place in a silence that suited us both.

That period marked the time when I started winning for real. I participated in all the races that were held in and around the city—those that could be entered for free—and I almost always came in first.

I soon felt the need to look for additional challenges and signed up for competitions open to athletes of southern Somalia. I won there too.

Everyone wondered how a skinny little girl, thin as a newly planted acacia, with legs that looked like olive branches, could possibly win. The fact is that I won, and that's that. I was faster than the others. At least the ones I happened to come across.

As the months passed, I realized that my specialty was the two hundred meters.

It was there that I was able to give my best. Though even in the four hundred meters I felt pretty confident. I didn't have muscles suitable for burning it all up in a hundred meters; I needed a little more distance to work off the fury and let Aabe's words take shape in my head. I couldn't do it right away, as soon as I took off. At the start, there was only drive.

After three or four seconds, however, the promise I'd made to Aabe emerged, and I would win.

Every time.

I wanted to become the strongest sprinter in all of Somalia, which meant going to run in the north, in Hargeysa, Somaliland. But it wasn't easy, because I needed someone to accompany me; then too I didn't have any money, and neither did Alì. Besides that, the north had declared itself independent, its people saying they hated the war; so anyone who wanted to go north, even just for a race, wasn't well regarded by the armed groups.

Moreover, just at the time when Nassir decided to follow Ahmed, everything changed in Mogadishu.

Al-Shabaab had gained a lot of power, and there was talk of opening the Islamic Courts. The alleged intent was to put an end to the war, but in reality it was merely a victory for the fundamentalists.

Within a few weeks, life in the city became impossible. Especially for women, though not only for them.

Then, in a single day, what should never happen anywhere happened.

In one day, a day like any other, with nothing on the horizon, no cataclysms or revolutions.

From one day to the next everything changed.

Overnight, listening to music was forbidden. You couldn't

listen anymore, either in the street or at home. The few who owned a radio had to keep the volume very low, because if a few notes were to drift outside they would risk a public lynching.

Overnight, all the movie theaters were shut down. Not that I'd ever had the money to go, but there had always been the hope that someday it would happen, and that alone was worth waiting for. Besides, there had always been some well-off classmate who would go there on Fridays with her family and come back with those wonderful, magical stories. Films created and fed people's dreams; that's why the theaters were shut down.

Overnight, men were obliged to wear long pants and could no longer be seen on the street in shorts. They also had to shave their heads completely or wear their hair long, Afro style, with long, full beards. Half measures were no longer acceptable.

Then there were the women. Women were no longer allowed to do anything; even walking down the street was risky. Trying it without a burka was a gamble that could cost you your life.

Overnight, the traditions of our country changed. The land of sunshine and color was transformed into an open-air training camp for extremists. None of our colorful *garbasar, jamar,* and *hijab* were permitted anymore. Suitable only for mopping the floor. We were obliged to wear the black burka, the garment that covers everything but your eyes.

But the worst thing of all, because it seemed like a punishment, was the decision to turn off the few streetlamps that at night lit up some of the city's squares and side streets.

In the evening, in fact, many people gathered in the squares under the streetlights to read. Very few had electricity at home. Instead of reading by the dim light of the *ferus*, many spent their evenings under the stars, reading a novel, an old newspaper, or maybe a letter or a love note.

Those places were our outdoor library. Now, like the library itself, everything was precluded, revoked, banned.

Al-Shabaab had managed to demolish the hope of an entire people. Everything that until that day had been difficult to achieve but possible had become impossible. Dreams, hopes, and freedom had all been wiped out in the blink of an eye.

Overnight.

One night Aabe could wear his khaki shorts, the kind from colonial days that the Italians had imported and that all men wore, especially on very hot days. The next morning it was forbidden: If he were to run into Al-Shabaab's watchdogs on the street, he'd risk being beaten in front of everyone.

It was the same for Hooyo, who had to wear a burka to go to work. She hated it, as we all did: We loved our bright colors, our orange, red, yellow, green, blue, and purple veils and *garbasar*, which for us had always represented the essence of the land and of femininity.

Overnight, however, the black burka for everyone.

For me and Hodan it was difficult.

For her, no more singing with the group, no more singing at all, not even hymns to freedom and peace.

And for me, no more running.

One of those evenings Hodan came by to eat at home with us. After supper Aabe and Hooyo said they wanted to talk to the two of us. Our brothers and sisters stayed outside to wash the bowls and rice pot; in silence we went to our parents' room.

Aabe, sitting on the only chair, eyed us nervously and kept

fiddling with his cane, shifting it from hand to hand. It was the first time we'd seen him so agitated. For her part, Hooyo—who was covered up to her head with the gauzy white veils that before then she'd never worn in the house—took a seat on the mattress and kept ironing out first her skirt, perfectly smooth over her lap, then the white cloth handkerchief she held.

Hodan and I gripped each other's hands tightly.

Without their even having to tell us, we were both afraid they might forbid us from doing what we loved. That they would tell us that everything had become too dangerous, that no one could afford to do what he wanted anymore. In part because family members would pay for it. Those were the methods Al-Shabaab used: exemplary punishment for siblings or parents to serve as a warning.

I was shaking and I felt feverish; I was freezing despite the high temperature. If Aabe ordered us to stop, what would we do? We could go cry in Hooyo's arms, pleading for mercy, as we had when we were little. But this time it would do no good.

We had only two choices: obey or disobey.

And disobeying would be like leaving home for good.

But Aabe was Aabe.

Without our having to say a word, nervously gripping the cane with those big hands sticking out from the sleeves of his beige cotton shirt, he had read our thoughts as they appeared on our faces.

He got up from his chair and slowly came over to us.

He rested a hand first on my forehead, then on Hodan's.

"My daughters, everything that up until yesterday was normal today is complicated."

His voice was serious. Hodan and I looked at each other. We knew what he would say. It was the end of our dreams. We could stop imagining some kind of future; reality had rained down like a bucket of ice water.

Together we lowered our eyes and stared at our bare toes, coated with white dust.

After a pause, Aabe continued. "But your mother and I believe that you should keep doing what you are doing, if what you are doing is your calling and makes you happy."

Hot, silent tears fell in unison from my eyes and Hodan's.

"Hooyo and I will always support you, Islamic Courts or not. Al-Shabaab or not."

Hooyo, on the mattress, was weeping the way she did when she didn't want anyone to notice. She kept blowing her nose repeatedly, as if she had a cold, but we'd known since we were little that there was nothing wrong with her.

"You just have to recognize that what you're doing is risky and not well regarded. Not only by the fundamentalists but also by many people who will let themselves be influenced and think that you are both crazy. Do you know this?"

"Yes," I replied, eyes still bright.

"Yes, Aabe, we know," Hodan said.

"So then you are free to build your future. Your mother and I are aware that each of you has a gift. Go and take what is coming to you, my daughters."

By that point we were sobbing. Aabe hugged us tightly and told us to leave them, that he and Hooyo wanted to be alone for a while.

Before we went out, however, he called Hodan back.

"Hodan . . ."

She turned, already at the door.

"Yes, Aabe?"

"Make sure that Hussein's father feels the same."

"Thank you, Aabe."

We went out to the courtyard, into the air and light, leaving our mother and our father in the darkness of their room, wondering if they had made the right decision.

CHAPTER 12

✻

NEVERTHELESS, in those weeks everything was changing no matter what. Our lives as Somalis were destined to be transformed forever.

One morning, without notice, Alì and his family moved out.

I got up at dawn along with my brothers and sisters, awakened by noises coming from the courtyard. We all stumbled out in our pajamas, barefoot and drowsy. I was just in time to see them pile into a green pickup truck towing a rusty trailer that Aabe Yassin had borrowed from someone, before they left for good. Gone, without our even knowing where.

Yassin, Alì, and his brothers had spent the night loading up the decrepit truck with boxes in which they had managed to pack away their entire lives.

The previous day the Hawiye clan, which we Abgal were part of, had announced that they had formed an alliance of sorts with Al-Shabaab; it seemed they didn't want to be at war for a change. This, however, meant that the Darod in our area were in danger, since Bondere was an Abgal district; Darod families had continued to live there only because they were protected by their Abgal friends. No one would have dared do any harm to Aabe Yassin; everyone knew that he was our father's best friend, that they were like brothers.

But that night, simultaneously, scores of families had made the same decision Alì's father had. Once again, overnight, Al-Shabaab had changed my life.

The morning was drenched with a surreal light. At dawn the air, misty with the sea's moisture, seemed inhabited by myriad swift ghosts. People from my district were moving to places as yet unknown. The important thing was to get away as quickly as possible. Leave their history behind.

Hooyo, like almost all of our neighbors, had not gone to work. Al-Shabaab's men might come and make an inspection, house by house. We all had to be present.

When I ran out to the pickup, Alì was sitting in the back next to the window, eyes downcast. Aabe Yassin was in front, next to the driver, who was a friend of his and Aabe's. The engine was already running. I rapped on the glass and Alì turned. A pall of despair had settled over his face like wax. He had no eyes anymore. His face was a waxen mask, a mask of absence.

He looked at me, but he was focused on a point in the sky instead of on me while I, on the other side of the glass, gestured for him to roll down the window. Alì didn't hear me; he seemed dazed. I turned to look behind me.

He was staring at the top of the eucalyptus.

Only when the pickup truck started to move did he look at me. He may have been crying. Finally.

Alì, his brothers, and Aabe Yassin had been part of my life since I was born and now, like ghosts, in a fraction of a second they were vanishing.

Hussein's family had made the same decision. They were also Darod, and there was no tolerance for mixed marriages anymore. Everything that had been gained in decades had gone up in smoke in a single day.

They had decided to leave, like most of the Darod.

Hodan, in the course of a few hours, found herself having to make a painful decision.

Leave or stay.

After an anguished night she'd decided to stay with us. What would become of her marriage was a question that there'd been no time to consider. Sometimes the weightiest decisions are carried along on the slight drift of a breath of air. And we with them, inadequate, flimsy. At least, that's what happened to us that morning.

A few hours after Alì's departure, Hodan returned home. With only the few belongings she had brought with her after the *aroos* ceremony. Not many, just the essentials.

When we saw her appear in the courtyard with the little red cardboard suitcase that many years ago had been Hooyo's, Hodan said simply: "I'm back. Hussein left."

Hooyo rushed to embrace her, and we all followed her.

In the blink of an eye I'd lost my best friend and gotten my sister back.

But fate could do whatever it wanted with me. I knew exactly where I was headed. The wind has always had a tough time with my skinny body. It's me who has always moved *it*, as I ran by. It was me who had learned to use the wind as a driving force behind my back, to make me fly.

What I did that morning was embrace Hodan, crying with joy and shedding the same bitter tears that were still flowing for Alì.

Then right away I started training again.

CHAPTER 13

✤

I HAD BEEN LEFT WITHOUT a coach at age fourteen and
six months away from the most important race of my life, the one
in Hargeysa. The one I had to win if I was to become the fastest
and be able to go to Djibouti to run in the name of my country
for the first time. The very thought of it made my head spin; I
had to do it at all costs.

There was no one to clock me anymore, no one to make me
do the exercises for my legs and arms. No one to check if I
cheated on the reps or the abdominals.

Every day since Ali's departure I had wondered where he
was, what he was doing. As I ran I heard his voice buzzing in my
ears. *Don't do this, don't do that. Lift your heels more, keep your
arms in close. Try to coordinate your breath with your stride. And
smile! When you reach the finish line, smile, Samia!*

I never did. I didn't care about smiling. By the end of a race I
was exhausted, and there were a ton of things I'd done wrong. I

knew there was room for improvement, and I just wanted to work on that. When I passed the finish line, I wasn't even able to savor the victory. I began thinking about the next race, mentally correcting my mistakes.

Besides that, I was also a little afraid. Afraid that there might be someone in the stands who didn't like young girls to flaunt themselves. Alì, on the other hand, pressured me each time and insisted that it was important to smile. "It's like acknowledging the spectators," he said.

In the evening before going to sleep, with the *ferus* still lit, I lost myself staring at Mo's photograph. I gazed at him and asked him questions. Said teased me, saying that I was talking to a piece of paper.

"Samia, are you still talking to that newspaper?"

"I'm not talking to any newspaper," I retorted irritably. Yet that's really just what I was doing: talking to a worn-out scrap of paper.

"Ink stains, you know, but it doesn't talk." Said kept it up.

When the others all laughed, I woke up from my trance. Then Hodan gave me a kiss on the forehead and told me not to get mad, that Said was only joking.

True, he was joking, but he was right.

I looked at Mo in that photo where he was about to cross the finish line, his eyes wide open and frenzied from the effort yet serene and satisfied with another victory, and I whispered to him to reassure me. To tell me that one day it would be the same for me. That I too would win with that look of hope and serenity in my eyes.

Still, winning serenely seemed unlikely to me. Each victory

was also a sin that I knew displeased a lot of people. Naturally I did everything I could not to let it bother me; I went my own way, not caring what others thought, not smiling either.

But the truth was that Ali's absence made it all seem less carefree, less of a game; running had taken on a different feel, even though Hodan was back to put me to sleep with her velvety voice.

During those months the only thing I did besides going to school was run. I trained as much as seven hours a day. I ran in the courtyard, and after curfew, as soon as I could, I went out and ran through the streets.

The burka over my head and under it the terry headband to soak up the sweat.

Running in that getup was impossible. I stumbled repeatedly in the long garment, and the heat buildup under that confining black garb brought me close to fainting each time.

But all I could think about was Hargeysa, the race of my life, the one that would change my destiny. I had to win; it was my only chance to become a professional, even though that word has never meant much in Somalia. No one has ever earned a red cent through sports. But I hoped that I would at least have the chance to compete in major races, to represent my country in the world and to run for the liberation of Somalia while Somalia thought I was playing by its rules.

Two days a week I went to help Hooyo at the vegetable stand, to earn a few shillings that would help pay for my bus ticket to Hargeysa. Hodan went with Hooyo on two other days and Ubah the last two, and they too gave me something whenever they could. Their contribution to freedom.

The Islamic Courts administration had prohibited Hodan and her group from rehearsing and playing in the city.

They could no longer go to the concert hall and were forced to meet in the cellar of a restaurant up north, toward the Shabelle River. If they were found again in the concert hall near the old port, they would be shot.

When I returned, drenched in sweat, from my run around the block at curfew, Hooyo looked at me strangely, as if I were a rare animal.

"Who did you take after?" she asked me, slipping off my burka and running a hand over my damp hair as she stood in the corner by the *burgico* preparing supper. Each time it was the same routine. As soon as she saw me duck in from under the red curtain, she smiled at me with her usual tenderness. Then, when I went over to her, she turned serious.

"Who did you take after, huh, little Samia?" she said in that gentle voice of hers. I'd grown as tall as her, and I noticed that her bright eyes, deep as a bottomless well, were being framed by wrinkles all around.

"I take after Aabe," I replied.

She looked at me, took my face between her hands, and said: "How beautiful you are, Samia. By now you're a woman. You're the most beautiful one in the family."

Then she folded the damp burka, untied the laces of my sneakers and told me to go rinse off and rest my feet.

It was like a ceremony. The disrobing of the beautiful, wacky daughter.

But at that time all I thought about was conserving my energy for the following day's training. I couldn't concentrate on anything else.

The day of my fifteenth birthday was two weeks before the race, and Said gave me a stopwatch.

I never knew where he got it or how much it cost. The fact is he came to me and said: "This is for you, warrior Samia."

It was the first time he'd called me that; usually Said came up with a hundred different names, all to make fun of me. But that day he called me "warrior," as Aabe sometimes called me, maybe because I was growing up: I was fifteen, and fifteen is a grown-up age. Then he said he hoped that stopwatch would someday mark the women's speed record for our country.

"I promise you, Said," I told him, kissing his cheek.

I had never had a stopwatch. Alì used to measure my time by calculating the seconds with his battered old wristwatch. The strap had been missing for a long time; only the dial remained. Until the day they stole that too from him.

He was on the corner of the national monument waiting for me to reappear from the narrow street across the way, when he was approached by a group of three Abgal boys whom he had never seen before; they must not have been from our neighborhood, and who knows what they were doing there? Alì was standing in the shade, leaning against the trunk of an acacia tree, when the three started insulting him.

"This Darod has a face just like a nigger," they said.

Alì, as always, didn't breathe a word; he looked them straight in the eye one by one.

"So this Darod doesn't talk. He must be so hungry he even ate his tongue." And the three morons burst out laughing.

Alì knew he wouldn't get very far with three against one. Besides, he was in an Abgal district, so he didn't have much hope. Remaining calm, he let the one who seemed like the leader get close enough, then suddenly, as swiftly as he had bitten the militiaman's hand that long-ago night, he kicked him on the shin. The guy doubled over in pain and Alì ran away fast. The other two ran after him for a while; then, being slower than him, they blew the whistle that thugs wear around their necks for times like these. *Tweeeeeee!* So loud it could be heard through half the city. Turning the corner, Alì found himself face to face with a man who stopped him, demanding to know why he was running and whether he had by chance stolen something, which was contrary to the law of the Koran. Right then the two guys showed up and told the man that Alì was a thief, that he'd stolen their money.

They beat him and took everything he had, which was only that strapless wristwatch. From then on we did without a watch.

Now, with Said's stopwatch, everything changed.

Who knew what Alì would have said. He'd have found it hard to believe that he could use a real timer. Being able to measure my times seemed impossible to me too.

Until that day all I had known was that I'd come in first.

I must have inherited the seed of madness from Aabe, in any case.

I was right to say that to Hooyo when she asked me. It was with my father's permission, in fact, that I went to the CONS stadium at night on the last three days before the Hargeysa race.

I had been asking him for years. Alì had told me many times about how he and his friends Amir and Nurud would sneak in and play soccer there when they were little. It had stuck in my mind. A time when I could use the stadium in peace.

Aabe had never given me permission to do it. Until those three days before the race, when I went to plead with him, and he relented.

"Thank you, Aabe. I'll be forever grateful to you," I told him, making sheep's eyes at him.

"I hope you'll be grateful when these three days are over, because it will mean that nothing happened to you," he replied worriedly.

The truth was that, even though it was pitch dark, this was the only time when there was no danger, because there was no one around and the evening curfew had already quieted things down.

I left the house around eleven o'clock, all covered up in my burka, and in half an hour, running through the most out-of-the-way streets, I was at the stadium.

I slipped through one of the holes in the fence, crossed the ticket-window area, climbed over a low gate that led to the central tunnel, and from there got in.

It was fantastic.

The scent of grass was overwhelming; my senses were completely engulfed by that sweet, subtle, pungent fragrance.

Having the empty stadium all to myself, illuminated only by the light of the moon, was as breathtaking as touching the star-studded sky.

I stopped at the edge of the tartan track on which I had won my first race and took off the onerous black burka. I folded it and left it on the ground. Then, as I took slow, deep breaths, just the idea of being in there at night produced a rush of adrenaline that energized me. I warmed up, taking long, unhurried strides that brought me to the center of the soccer field. From there, for a few seconds that lasted an eternity, I savored the sight of the deserted stadium.

Not a soul.

Only me, my breath, and the moon. And the scent of the grass, heady, all around me.

I pretended that there was peace outside, that this was a minor infraction and that I wasn't risking anything.

It was there, on those nights, three days before the most important race of my life, that I discovered that I could run a hundred meters in 16.32 seconds and two hundred meters in 32.90 seconds. I had thought I was faster, but I wasn't. Said's stopwatch had revealed a bitter truth. My times were way over the world records; like it or not, I would have to improve. I had no choice but to improve.

On all three of those nights Aabe was there waiting for me at the exit to take me home safe and sound. On the way back, covered by the burka but skipping joyfully, I spelled out everything I had to do to improve. He kept looking around nervously, and every so often he would stop and threaten me with his cane, telling me to settle down and not attract attention, or he'd bop me on the head. I laughed; I knew we shouldn't be out and about at that hour, but I was happy.

The sudden freedom, the empty stadium, the full moon, the scent of grass filled me with irrepressible euphoria.

Aabe got mad and told me to quiet down.

But all I could think about was the race.

Three days later I left for the north.

CHAPTER 14

❋

THE BUS TRIP TO HARGEYSA made me feel like a celebrity. I was by myself and the ticket was expensive, the equivalent of sixty U.S. dollars—being able to buy it was a miracle in itself.

I had never been on a bus. Everything was very comfortable, the seats soft and roomy, covered in gray velvet, and there was background music. The driver wore a dark blue uniform and he was very kind. When he saw me get on alone, wearing the tracksuit that Aabe had gotten hold of somewhere and given me for the occasion, he must have thought I was a famous athlete. He looked at me and greeted me the way you regard and address a person worthy of respect.

"Good morning, *abaayo*," he said to me as I climbed in. "Have a good trip."

"Thank you" was all I managed to say, I was so excited.

The journey took almost a whole day.

I felt like one of those tiny birds that beat their wings so rapidly that all you see is a blur; the birds look like they're suspended in the air, dangling somehow from an invisible thread. I was so impatient that I couldn't sit still. I must have gotten up a hundred times with the excuse of stretching my legs. When we stopped to get out and eat something or go to the bathroom, I couldn't wait to get moving again.

We reached our destination at seven the next morning, as the sun was rising. I hadn't slept for even one minute.

I got off the bus with the strange feeling of being in a country at peace.

The fact that there were no armed guards at the station, that there were no traces of guns or camouflage uniforms, and that outside there were no bullet holes in the walls didn't seem real. I felt disoriented. Like an animal that has spent its entire life in a cage and suddenly finds itself free, the cage door open. I was struck by a feeling of extreme euphoria, which instead of spurring me on at that moment immobilized me. I was tempted to turn around, get back on the bus, and return home to my natural setting, where freedom was measured by counting land mines and mortar rounds. That morning at dawn, with the sun peeking shyly through the cracks between the station's wooden roof and walls, I thought that too much freedom so unexpectedly isn't good for people; they aren't used to it.

I sat on a metal bench beside a newspaper stand and waited a bit. The news vendor was opening up just then, his face still sleepy.

With the few shillings I had I bought a *shaat* in the only bar that was open. The heat flowed from my hands to my throat and from there, after a while, finally reached my head.

I made my way to the stadium on foot.

I had all the time in the world, plus I had to loosen up my

joints after all those hours with my knees bent, not being able to straighten them.

The city at peace seemed like a miracle to me. Being able to go around without a burka, being able to walk or even shout in the middle of the street. Being able to stop someone and talk to him. The idea of being able to do all those things made my head spin.

After an hour I reached the stadium; it was now eight o'clock. The guard behind the gate was moved to take pity on me. When he heard where I'd traveled from, he opened the gate with a big key, let me in, and even found me a shady spot where I could rest.

I tried to lie down on the grass surrounding the track, in front of the stands, but sleep was the last thing on my mind.

I was quivering like the strings of a *shareero*, the instrument that Hussein played in Hodan's group.

At ten they opened the gates and the first runners arrived with their coaches. Only then, unhurriedly, did they set up the tables for those who had signed up.

I was the first to present myself.

The lady in charge looked at me questioningly and asked me my name. I answered her, terrified that somehow, between Mogadishu and Hargeysa, my name might have been lost along with my registration and that I had come all that way for nothing.

But the lady looked me up and down and only asked: "Did you sleep, child?"

"Yes, of course I slept. How could I run if I hadn't rested, *abaayo*?" I replied, candid as a lily.

"All right, then go rinse your face afterward. There's a fountain over there."

"Thank you, *abaayo*."

"What's your name, child?"

"Samia Yusuf Omar," I said, all in one breath.

The lady opened the register and searched. Endless seconds went by. "I come from Mogadishu, *abaayo*," I added.

"Samia Yusuf Omar from Mogadishu . . . Here it is."

I signed the book and she gave me the bib with my number. My first bib.

I was signed up for the women's one-hundred-meter and two-hundred-meter races.

My number was 78.

I had to wait another two hours before running. I didn't know what to do with myself.

Fortunately, the women competed before the men.

I exchanged a few words with a couple of girls, but I couldn't get too distracted. I was there to win, not to chat. I kept looking around; I couldn't help it. Everything was new to me. It was my first time in the north, my first real race.

I was surely the youngest. No one would have bet a shilling on me.

After a while, when my impatience had reached its peak, I took the path of least resistance. I lay down on the grass and waited for time to pass. Surrounded by that sweet, enveloping scent.

Until the moment came.

My opponents didn't seem very intimidating. They were older than me, but they didn't have the fervent eyes of real athletes. Right away I had the feeling that I could come in first.

In a little less than two hours I won the two qualifying rounds in the heats, one after the other.

Before I knew it, I found myself in the final, with a lot less breath, a great deal of pain in my quadriceps, and two races behind me. One in the hundred meters and one in the two hundred.

The first-place finishers from each heat were admitted to the final.

The first of the finals was the two hundred meters. My legs were stiff as boards from the overexertion; I was twice as exhausted as the others because I was the only one to run both races.

But that only made me more driven. If I had come this far, I might even win.

I bent over the starting blocks and at the signal took off like a rocket, my eyes only on the finish line.

In my head, as always, were the voices of Aabe and Alì, shouting at me to run.

And I ran.

I crossed the finish line first.

It was a huge thrill, the greatest feeling of liberation.

Number one.

I was the fastest runner of my country in the two hundred meters. Something that I was barely able to absorb.

I didn't have much time to let it sink in, however. In ten minutes the hundred-meter final, the most important race, would be run.

The spectators in the stands began to make themselves heard for the first time. Some shouted, cheering us on.

As we headed for the starting blocks, the girl in the lane next to mine pointed to a small group of people in the stands who were trying to get my attention. When I looked over, they began clapping and rooting for me. I had fans.

I raised my arm and waved at them.

When the starting gun went off, I again heard only the voices of Aabe and Alì in my head. *Run, little warrior. Run and smile at the finish line!*

I burned those hundred meters like I'd never done before.

The girls to my right and to my left were slower than I was; instantly I was two steps ahead of them. Out of the corner of my eye I saw that there was only one runner, in the first lane, who was even with me. In the last ten meters I poured out everything that had brought me to that track.

The strain and effort, the training, the commitment, the fears and frustrations that I'd experienced for at least seven years. I looked back at Mogadishu like a cage from which I had finally been able to escape and run free.

And I won. Again.

When I reached the finish, I felt like a cricket that for weeks has been prevented from jumping, caught and kept in a box, as kids do in Mogadishu. They keep it in their pocket; then, after days, they release it, and the cricket jumps a long distance. They have jumping contests for crickets that have been penned up, and they bet on them. I felt like one of those confined crickets. I kept jumping left and right; I could have reached the sky. And the beauty of it was that we were in Hargeysa, there was no war, there were no Al-Shabaab men.

Here, at last, I could jump and celebrate in peace.

And I could smile too.

I smiled at everyone and I shook hands with those who came up to meet me. If Alì had seen me, he would have been so happy he'd have cried like a little girl. I hadn't seen him in six months, and in my heart I dedicated the victory to him, to my coach. To the one who had made me become an athlete. And who was my best friend.

That day was the first time I saw my official times, posted in large letters on an electronic scoreboard: 15.83 for the hundred meter, and 32.77 for the two hundred.

There was still a lot of room for improvement, but I had won. I was the fastest woman in my country.

And I had earned the right to run in the race to be held in Djibouti three months from now. My first international competition.

On the trip back I slept for twenty hours straight. We left in the evening and would not arrive until the following evening. I never opened my eyes, not even once; I didn't even get out of the bus to go to the bathroom.

I had my two medals around my neck, safely tucked under my T-shirt, where I still wore the bib with 78, my lucky number.

Only for the first hour did I feel like a bomb about to explode. An elderly lady sitting beside me was trying to read a book by the dim light that filtered through the window, and I felt the irresistible urge to tell her everything that had happened to me, minute by minute. Every so often I tried to start a conversation. There was no way; she never raised her eyes from those pages.

Afterward I began to crumble. I hadn't slept in two days and I plunged into a deep, deep sleep. I fell asleep with my hand over the medals, grasping the jacket of my tracksuit.

At the bus station in Mogadishu, everything was the same as I had left it. For me centuries had passed; I had traveled to the other side of the world and had become someone else. Yet in a flash I found myself back where I'd started, as if nothing had happened: the usual troubled faces, sunken and anxious, the usual rifles over the shoulders, the usual stained, crumpled uniforms, salvaged from who knows where.

Outside the station Aabe was waiting for me.

There was no need for me to say anything; he read it all on my face. I leaped at him, arms around his neck, and covered him with kisses.

On the way back I was obsessed by the idea of running into Al-Shabaab patrols. I used the technique that Hodan had taught me as a little girl, which I had later taught Alì: invisibility. It had always worked. Except for the time with the two boys and Ahmed. It was simple: If you think you're invisible, Hodan had told me, then you really become invisible. It was the way we went around the city; it was the secret that we'd always used, even Alì and I when we went running at curfew or when we ventured out to the beach when we were little.

Now I used it for me and Aabe. So that the bubble of invisibility might protect us from everything and everyone forever and ever.

It was past eleven when we got home. Everyone had already eaten, but they had kept a plate of *kirisho mirish* and sweet sesame cakes for me.

Hooyo, crying as usual, said she was proud of me. Even Hodan joined in with Hooyo's tears, and my other brothers and sisters came up with a song in my honor.

That evening, the night of the victory, everything was perfect.

I was transformed.

For the first time I felt grown up, like an adult. On top of that, I knew I was a champion, and buried somewhere in the pit of my stomach was the conviction that one day I would win the Olympics. And that when that day came, I would indeed lead the resurgence of Muslim women.

I watched my siblings sing as if I were in a bubble of silence. I could see their mouths moving, but I couldn't hear their voices.

The absence of Alì, his brothers, and Aabe Yassin was palpable. Maybe that's why my family was more emotional than usual.

Alì, my coach, wasn't there, and for the first time in my life I wept inconsolably.

Hodan and Hooyo thought I was crying for joy over the victory. No, that night in the courtyard, in front of my entire family celebrating in my honor, I cried because I had grown up and because I missed Alì. The one person in the world who had devoted himself to training me so that I might win the race that I had won that day. And who didn't even know it.

Before going to sleep I hung the two medals on a nail in the wall beside the mattress. Next to Mo Farah's face.

Who knows, maybe even Mo could see them.

From Europe, from London. From far, far away.

Who knows, maybe he might decide to send me a note of encouragement for what was to come, for the upcoming race in Djibouti, for instance.

Then, before I dropped off to sleep, Hodan's velvet voice sang me a wonderful, glorious victory song.

CHAPTER 15

※

A MONTH LATER, with the unconditional finality with which everything had now started happening in my life, Aabe left us forever. With the swiftness and inevitability with which events were taking place, my guiding light was also gone. One moment everything was as it always was. And the next moment nothing was the same anymore. As of that day, darkness fell.

That morning, as he often did, Aabe had gone to the Bakara market to meet a few friends and do some shopping. Someone, his face concealed, came up behind him and shot him. Just like that, for no reason. An act that only took a moment. Of no consequence to any onlooker, inconspicuous amid all the frenzied hawking and shouting. Given the general indifference, the shadowy figure slipped away without even causing a stir. No one made a move; very few had even noticed.

Bakara was the most dangerous place in the city. Packed with people coming and going at all hours hunting for items to buy and sell, hoping to make a profit or just waste time. Every corner

brimming with color—blue, green, red, yellow, white, black—
the colors of the fabrics, the spices, the fruits and vegetables. And
above all teeming with hands, legs, feet, faces, eyes darting rapidly from this to that, the reek, the odors, the ooze. Littered with
spit, banana peels, apple cores, watermelon rinds, the remains of
apricots and peaches. That's Bakara, a hellhole. Because it was so
congested, it had always been the most unsafe place.

But until that day it had been the place where *other people*
died. The site of deaths that no one cared about.

The clans' militiamen, or Al-Shabaab's men, might place a
bomb inside a shopping bag slung over a woman's back. One
would drop the bomb in as he passed by. Then, from a distance
away, another one pressed a button. And *boom*.

Twenty people in one fell swoop. Or thirty.

Children, women, elderly people.

No one gave a damn about it. Activity around the corpses
stopped just long enough for everything to go back to normal. It
was always someone else who died, someone else who left parents, children, relatives, and friends.

That day, however, that "someone else" suddenly touched us,
and death took on its full significance.

That day it was Aabe Yusuf.

Our father.

Gone.

Forever.

After that night Hodan and I no longer slept on our mattresses but in the big bed with Hooyo. Aabe's body had been laid
out on a wooden table covered with a cloth, on view in the courtyard for twenty-four hours, for the public to pay its respects. Our

mother spent nearly the entire time standing there welcoming the people who came, her hand in the hand of her dead husband. I, however, didn't even look at him. I wanted to keep my memory of him intact forever.

Said couldn't stop crying while Hodan entered into a silence that she broke only at night, in bed.

She slept between me and Hooyo and sang us to sleep with hymns that accompanied Aabe's Journey, songs that spoke to us with his voice, as if he were with us and were telling us that it was all the fault of the warlords and fundamentalists that he had left us alone. She sang clenching her fists.

We lay hand in hand staring at the ceiling, Hodan in the middle with one hand in mine and the other in Hooyo's, and as she sang in that strained voice she almost crushed our knuckles.

When we buried him, there was a stream of people with us. Everyone introduced himself as Aabe's best friend.

Aabe was gone and, like it or not, life had to go on.

His absence in the smallest everyday actions plunged me into a state of furious rage that intensified rather than destroyed my urge to run and to win. What's more, it made me invincible and unassailable. Nothing could ever hurt me anymore. They had already taken Aabe from me; no one could ever again find fault with what I did.

My grief was so great that I did not fear the worst. Often as I ran, I found myself crying like mad. When I came home and he wasn't sitting in the courtyard, I burst into sobs. In the evening, after dinner, we missed his deep voice and his jokes. Said tried, but the void seemed even more painful.

In those days and weeks I felt an obligation to complete what I had started in the name of the invincibility that Aabe had bestowed on me. Sometimes as I ran, my mind wandering on its own, I caught myself imagining the most absurd, unthinkable things: that Aabe had been taken from us just to allow me to run freely, protected by his death, which had brought vengeance to our family.

But as soon as I stopped and pulled myself together, I realized that I was just being foolish.

The world had lost its colors, its scents, its sounds. From that day on, everything was dulled, murky, like the wax of Alì's face that morning. It was as if I had entered an endless tunnel, the space between its walls barely wider than me, and all I could do was run, run as fast as I could, looking for a way out.

And in fact, during the two months before the race in Djibouti, I ran to the point of collapse.

Each time I trained I heard in my head the words that Aabe had told me the morning of my first big race: *You're a little warrior running for freedom, whose efforts alone will redeem an entire people.*

Those words pushed me to the extreme.

I trained in the courtyard with the weights; then at night I would sneak away to the CONS stadium, covered by the burka, and practice starts, sprints, lunges, reps. I felt invincible. Every day I would go on like that, six, seven, eight hours straight.

Until I collapsed on the ground, exhausted. Without Alì to grip my wrists and pull me back up.

So usually I sprawled on the patchy grass of the soccer field and lay there for minutes at a time, gazing at the sky.

I liked to picture myself from up above, from where Aabe was looking down on me, like a point in the center of a huge rectangle.

There was only the grass prickling my back, the cool, fresh evening air, the sky full of stars, my heavy breathing, and myself.

After a while everything became silent, my body began to unwind, my legs and back relaxed, my breath settled down.

Then I would take a deep breath and hold it for a while; I'd discovered that the effort kept the tears from coming. I stayed like that for as long as I could, my cheeks puffed out like a carp, so filled with air they nearly burst.

Until it was time to come back to earth, to get up and put on that horrible black garment that covered me from head to toe.

And return home, slowly, breathing through my nose and trying to keep my head empty of any thoughts.

May a thousand pounds of putrid shit fall on your heads and bury you forever.

CHAPTER 16

❉

ONE DAY WHEN I came home from school, there was a man talking with Hooyo in the courtyard who claimed to be from the Olympic Committee. Somewhat balding, with broad shoulders that spoke of a lean, athletic physique.

He was wearing a suit and tie, which immediately made me mistrustful, because only bridegrooms, politicians, and business-men dressed that way. But then he told me that he knew about my win in Hargeysa and that Abdi Bile himself, the great cham-pion from the eighties, would be glad to meet me.

"Okay, but when?" I asked.

"Right away, if you'd like," he replied calmly as he adjusted his tie. "By the way, I haven't yet introduced myself. I am Xas-san. Xassan Abdullahi."

I looked at Hooyo and Hodan, who nodded yes without speak-ing. I could go if I wanted to. Hodan, however, would come with me.

"We're only too pleased to have your sister come as well," the man said in his equable way. "Let's go. I have the car parked down the street." He seemed like a British gentleman or like someone who had traveled a lot in his youth or had lived abroad a great deal.

Hodan and I looked at each other. For the first time in our lives we would ride in a car!

We left the courtyard and the man led us to the car. It was a red Honda sedan. He opened the back door and we got in. It was very cold inside, because of the air-conditioning. It felt like being surrounded by ice. Then too the black leather seats made a crackling noise every time we moved. Seen through the windows of the car, the city looked different, both smaller and more impoverished. The people along the streets whom I had seen a million times seemed even more like good-for-nothing idlers.

We arrived in twenty minutes or so. It was the first time I had set foot in the headquarters of the National Olympic Committee.

Inside there were men and boys, some wearing the tracksuit of Somalia's national team, others dressed stylishly like Xassan. He went into a room, politely telling us to wait for him outside. On the walls were lots of photographs of athletes. Hodan and I kept looking around, feeling ill at ease.

As we lingered in the hall, a young man wearing Somalia's blue tracksuit came up and showed us to a place where we could sit down. It was a small room with more photographs. After a while, another man appeared at the door: white hair, jacket and tie, and a pleasant face. Hodan and I were as awkward as two little girls on the first day of school.

"Let's go to my office," he said with a big smile, motioning us out. We entered the office and were seated in two black leather chairs in front of his desk. A nameplate on the door read DR. DURAN FARAH, VICE PRESIDENT. Along the walls, shelves held numerous trophies. He took a box of chocolates out of a drawer and offered them to us. I'm not a sweets lover, except for sesame paste, but Hodan is, and she took two. After asking us how we were and exchanging a few words with me, he said they knew that I'd won an important race and they thought they could try to make me into a real athlete.

"But I'm already a real athlete," I replied, digging my heels in under the chair.

"Let's say you're on your way to becoming one." He smiled.

"But I won the race in Hargeysa. I'm the fastest woman in the country," I insisted. I would have punched him there on the spot if he'd continued questioning my ability.

The man looked at me with his head slightly tilted; then he again displayed his white teeth in a smile. "Among the amateurs, Samia. For now, only among the amateurs."

It was the first time he'd said my name, and I liked the way he pronounced it, with a drawn-out *a*. "Saaamìa," just as Aabe used to say it. I drove the thought of my father out of my head. "Do you want to become a professional?" he asked then, breaking through the drift of my memories.

I didn't answer right away because I couldn't believe my ears.

"Do you want to become a part of our Olympic team?" Duran repeated in that gentle voice of his.

At that point he could just as well have asked me to jump off a mountain or swim up the Shabelle River and I would have done so without a second's hesitation.

Six weeks later I was back on a bus. Only this time I hadn't had to help Hooyo for months to pay for my ticket.

A bus to Djibouti.

With me was Xassan.

Overhead, a Somalia duffel bag.

On me, a blue Somalia tracksuit.

It was all so perfect that every morning since meeting Xassan, I had gone to Hooyo and asked her to pinch my cheek to make sure it wasn't a dream.

It prompted the first smile of the day from her, those mornings when her eyes were still swollen from crying all night, thinking about Aabe.

On that bus I felt like Florence Griffith Joyner, the fastest woman of all time, the perfect athlete, whose name had been engraved in my memory the first time I'd heard it on the radio at Taageere's: Poor man, I always made him tune in to the sports station.

I was wearing the color of my country, the blue of the sky and sea, and I felt like the strongest sprinter in the world. I would so much have liked Aabe to be with me. Sometimes I thought that even Alì would have been enough, if I couldn't have Aabe back. From their eyes I would have been sure that everything that was happening to me was real. Papa would have whispered gently: "I told you, my little warrior." And that would have eliminated any doubt. Then he would have kissed me on the head, though I would have had to be the one to bend down, since I was taller now; I could no longer sit on his lap. And he would have said simply: "Go. Go and win."

The two drivers spelled each other several times, and I slept almost the entire way. There was Xassan to watch over me.

After a twenty-eight-hour trip, we arrived in Djibouti.

We would rest up the night before the race in order to be in top form. Sleeping in a hotel was one of those things—like riding in a car, traveling by bus, wearing the Somalia uniform—that had always seemed impossible to me. Yet it was all real. The light of my good fortune had been lit somewhere. Maybe it was Aabe who turned it on, in a secret place known only to him.

The hotel wasn't fancy—it wasn't even all that clean—but it was what our poor Olympic Committee could afford. Still, I had a room all to myself with a bed, a mattress, and carpeting on the floor. Though the surroundings were a little shabby thanks to time and cigarette burns, there were no nocturnal animals, none of the spiders or cockroaches that drove Ubah crazy (sometimes at night she'd start hopping around like a cricket and would wake us all up with her shrieks). There were no awful things. Only nice things. But the best thing of all was the bathroom. I had never had one in my entire life. We'd always used the common toilet in the courtyard. A hut with a big hole in the ground that was emptied each week. We've never had running water; my brothers went to get water from the well every night before supper. By contrast, here in the hotel in Djibouti I had a bathroom all to myself.

A sink with a faucet. It was a little dirty, and the steady trickle had left a rusty stain, but if I turned the faucet on, as much water as I wanted came out.

A bathtub with a shower. I could stand under it and turn on the hot water and wash as long as I wanted without Hooyo saying anything.

And there was a toilet bowl for doing your business. I could pull the chain to flush it and the stink disappeared.

After ten minutes I felt like going down to the reception desk and calling Taageere to have him pass me Hodan so I could tell her everything. But I would save the news until I returned.

That night, on that mattress, I slept so soundly that it seemed like forever.

The next morning we took the bus straight to the stadium. It was a real stadium; I had never seen one like it. Not even the one in Hargeysa had looked anything like it. This was an honest-to-goodness stadium, even bigger than the new one we had in Mogadishu: the one occupied by the militias and their tanks. It was enormous, huge. And its stands soared several tiers high, packed with people in constant motion, chanting, cheering, clapping, or whistling.

I was all worked up, but Xassan was serene; he appeared to be in perfect command of the situation.

The other athletes seemed much taller and more muscular than I. And they were dressed better too. I was wearing a used tracksuit. And I would run in my own T-shirt, my own shorts. The terry headband from Aabe. Somalia couldn't afford more, and I didn't ask for more; what I had already seemed like a lot to me. The other women, however, wore high-tech tank tops and matching shorts. Brand-name shoes and socks.

It all made me uncomfortable; I felt out of place, inferior. Xassan, on the other hand, remained composed, as if he were used to it.

I just had to keep in mind that, like the other women, I was there to represent my country and that I was being asked to give it my all. And to do so in one shot: There were no qualifying rounds; we gave it our best in two hundred meters.

"Run as fast as you can," Xassan said while we waited at the edge of the track for them to call our heat.

"I'll try."

"Samia." I looked at him. He lowered his voice almost to a whisper. "You won't win today. You won't even come close, but show me what you can do. Show me you're not afraid of the track, the spectators, or your opponents."

I squinted as if the sun were in my eyes, forcing myself not to lower my gaze. "I'm never afraid, Xassan," I lied.

"Good girl. Don't be afraid today either. You'll see: Everything will go as it should." Then he walked off toward the end of the course, carrying the tracksuit that I had worn during the warm-up, and I was left alone to await the call.

As I'd done in Hargeysa, and as I now did at night in Mogadishu, I lay down on the ground. It had become a ritual. I loved to feel the grass prickling my back and have its subtle, pungent scent in my nose. A ritual that I hoped would bring me luck here too.

When I heard my name on the loudspeaker, I got up. Head down, focused, I went to my block. I was starting in the fifth lane.

In much less time than I would have expected, the starting gun was fired.

Boom.

I gave it my all, everything I had.

The others were simply faster than me; Xassan was right. I pushed to the limit, but there was nothing more I could do. Though I spurred my muscles to the bursting point, it was no use.

I finished sixth out of eight.

It had not gone well, yet I was still nearly ecstatic.

Aabe had watched me from the place where he was, and he was as joyful as I was; I felt it. Maybe even more so. His little warrior had run and given it her all, even though she hadn't won. But winning really didn't matter to him—I knew that. All he wanted was for me to push myself to the limit.

Two days later, at home, I regaled them all with my stories. The trip, the hotel, the stadium, the opponents, the size of the crowd, Xassan, all of it. I went to each of my siblings and insisted on repeating the whole account. I was all revved up.

Hodan, on the other hand, seemed strange.

She was happy for me, but I sensed a distance. It felt like she had something to tell me and was just waiting for the right time, even though she was trying hard not to let me notice. But between us there could be no secrets. I knew everything about her, even the slightest vibe, just as she knew everything about me.

It wasn't until just before going to bed that she told me she needed to talk to me. That she had made a decision.

I didn't know what she was talking about.

At first, through tears and sobs, she just kept repeating that she had made up her mind.

I took her by the hand and led her to our room, to our mattresses, our natural place. Nothing could be so terrible; we had already experienced all the pain imaginable with Aabe's death.

But Hodan kept sobbing and saying that she shouldn't be crying, that it was actually a positive thing, a good thing. For her, at least.

Then she told me.

She could no longer stay in our country; the sense of guilt for what had happened to Aabe was killing her. The only thing she could do was leave. She had waited to tell me, waited until I ran the race in Djibouti and came back happy, at least, if not a winner.

But she had already made up her mind two months ago. And I hadn't noticed a thing. Aabe's death on the one hand and the Olympic Committee on the other must have blinded me to the world around me if I hadn't realized that Hodan was brooding over such an important decision.

She kept saying that it was all her fault that our father was gone, but I knew that it was my fault too. Indeed, in my heart I believed that Aabe had been taken away so that I could run in peace.

Something must be wrong, Hodan said, if Aabe had always urged us to follow our instinct for freedom, had actually nurtured it in us, yet that same instinct had first crippled him and then killed him.

I begged her; I tried in every way I could to remind her of what we had promised each other years ago, a promise that still meant something to me: that we would never leave our country, that we would stay and change it. I tried telling her that maybe Aabe had sacrificed himself for us, to allow us to realize our dreams more freely. Which were also his dreams for the liberation of our country.

"Don't you remember what we told each other in bed, almost every night?" I said, tears streaming down my face.

"Of course I remember my songs." Her voice was hard, turned to stone.

"So how can you want to leave now?"

"Everything has changed, Samia."

"What's changed? There's war now and there was war before." I was angry, my hands twitching.

"Now there's Al-Shabaab." Hodan, unlike me, was composed. "Before, there was respect; now there's only violence."

"We have to make a greater effort," I insisted, pounding a fist on the mattress.

"No, our efforts will only lead to more violence. Don't you see, Samia?"

No, not only didn't I understand, but I didn't believe it. "I have to stay here and continue running; this is my destiny. I have to win the Olympics, Hodan. I have to show the whole world that we can change. I have to keep the promise I made to Aabe. . . . This is what I must do."

"You have a talent, Samia," Hodan said quietly, putting a hand on my shoulder, "and it's right that you continue to follow your path." She dried her tears and blew her nose. She looked like Hooyo when she pretended she wasn't moved. In that position, in that light, Hodan had our mother's face. She had become a woman, and I hadn't realized it. "What *I* dream of today, though, is to be free. Right now, unconditionally. I dream of having a family, as I could not do with Hussein. I dream that my children may grow up in peace. The war took away my husband, and I don't even know for sure where he is." She paused. "At this point I just need a new life, Samia."

"I dream of being a free woman too, but I'm going to realize that dream here," I said, shrugging her hand off my shoulder.

"Not me, Samia." She was silent for perhaps a minute, but to me it seemed like a year or a millennium. "I'm leaving for Europe. Maybe I'll get to England, like Mo Farah." She tilted her chin up toward the photo, which still hung where I'd stuck it that long-ago night, next to the two medals from Hargeysa. "Or maybe Sweden or Finland."

There was nothing more to say.

Hodan had made up her mind.

All I could do was use the time remaining before she left to resign myself to it, so I wouldn't be unprepared and distraught when the time came and we had to separate.

I was beginning to think that the more I achieved in running, the more I lost in life.

CHAPTER 17

❁

AFTER THE RACE IN DJIBOUTI, the Olympic Committee gave me a pair of running shoes. The kind with cleats in the soles. But the thing that most changed my life was that I could go running at the stadium during the day, in sunlight.

Each moon that passed, however, was for me one less moon before Hodan's departure. In the months that remained before our separation, I continued training as much as before, if not more. The tunnel I had entered with Aabe's death had become even more endless. All I could do was lower my head and try to run my way out of it. I had just one goal: to keep from thinking and in that way qualify for the Beijing Olympics in 2008. As I had promised Aabe. I knew it all depended on me, on the times I'd be able to achieve on the track.

I dropped out of school because we couldn't afford it anymore. The longer the war went on, the less money people had. The little money that Hooyo managed to bring home was needed for food.

Truthfully, I wasn't too sorry, because that way I could run both in the morning and in the afternoon. By the time I got home in the evening, I was wiped out, but I didn't care; I collapsed on the mattress before the others went to bed and woke up the next morning after a deep, restful sleep, full of energy.

I also tried, in my heart, to get used to the loss of Hodan's singing, her caresses, the hand that squeezed mine before going to sleep. And she did the same.

For the second time we prepared to say good-bye. But this time we wouldn't be seeing each other during the day at school.

We spent that period before the separation in a state of pathological attachment and, at the same time, of morbid rejection. If one of us came home and the other wasn't there, we would search for hours and then, once found, not talk to each other. Or we fought as we had never done before, and when Hooyo or Said stepped in to have us make up, we'd burst into tears and hug each other tightly.

It was our tormented way of putting distance between us.

Two months later, in October 2007, Hodan left one night to set out on the Journey. She'd filled a small backpack with a few things; she had with her the shillings needed for the bus to Hargeysa, the requisite first stop for leaving the country, and not much more.

Without saying a word to anyone, she turned up that night ready to leave. She preferred to say good-bye without much fuss, especially for Hooyo's sake. I wasn't surprised; it was just like Hodan.

That way there was no time for lengthy good-byes and weeping. We held each other tight, and we all kissed her, Hooyo last of all. Before letting her go, Hooyo gave her a folded white hand-kerchief that held one of the small shells from the jar that Aabe had given her when they became engaged. Our portable sea, the one we would listen to when we were little. Hooyo tied the hand-kerchief to Hodan's wrist.

Then Hodan was gone.

She left on foot, alone, to walk to the bus station.

Without even knowing what she would do once she got to Hargeysa. But that too was just like Hodan.

The Journey is something we've all had in our heads from the time we were born. Everyone has friends and relatives who did it, or who in turn know someone who did it. It's like a mythological creature that can just as easily lead to salvation or death. No one knows how long it might take. If you're lucky, two months. If you're unlucky, as long as a year, or even two.

Ever since we were children, the Journey has been a favorite topic of conversation. Everyone has told stories about relatives who reached their destinations in Italy, Germany, Sweden or England. Scores of trailer trucks with men who perished, scorched by the sun, in the oven of the Sahara. Human traffickers and appalling Libyan prisons. Not to mention the numbers of travelers who die during the most difficult leg: crossing the Mediterranean from Libya to Italy. Some say tens of thousands, others say hundreds of thousands. We've been hearing these stories, these unsubstantiated numbers, since the time we were born. Because those who make it there always say the same thing when they call home: *I can't tell you what the Journey was like. It was horrific, that's for sure, but words can't describe it.* That's why it's always shrouded in absolute mys-tery. A mystery that for some is necessary in order to reach safety.

Hodan, like all those who leave, knew only that she would get to northern Europe. That somehow she would cross those ten thousand kilometers. She would find a good man, she would get married again, have children and live a happy life. Every month she would send money home, a little for Mama and a little for me, to allow me to run, and she would wait until she was settled enough to be able to pay for the Journey for us too. That was what everyone did, and that much she knew, that much she had been told. Everything in between wasn't worth thinking about.

And so, with a certain foolhardy unawareness, she left.

We, of course, were greatly concerned. We knew we could not expect any news, except occasionally, and this, rather than leaving us in the hands of blind hope, made us even more anxious.

Every so often, when she managed to find a phone somewhere, she would call us. Said had bought a cell phone, and we passed it around so Hodan could exchange a few words with each of us. At times, if there was an Internet connection available, like when she was in Sudan and then in Libya, we set a time an hour later when we would write to each other for hours. I went to Taageere's, the only place close to home with a computer. We did this a few days in a row sometimes, when she was forced to stop someplace to wait until Said, Abdi, Shafici, or Hooyo managed to scrape together enough money to send her to pay the traffickers for another leg of the Journey. Hodan awaited the day when she would go and withdraw the money at the money-transfer booth the way one awaits death.

Though she did all she could to hide the fact, I knew that the Journey terrified her. How could it not? She was alone, she had no money, and she was prey to human traffickers called *hawaian*, beasts, who beat their victims like animals if they didn't pay.

Sometimes she wrote that she was afraid, so afraid. Sometimes she couldn't help telling me. And even though I was more afraid than she was, I would write: "Never say you're afraid, *abaayo*, because if you do, the things you dream of won't come true."

It was what Aabe had taught me when I was little. You must never say you're afraid, because if you do, fear—that vile, evil monster—will never go away.

"Never say you're afraid, little Samia," Aabe used to tell me, and I repeated the words now to Hodan. "Don't say it."

Because if you do, you won't get to Europe.

But, as Allah willed, Hodan was among the lucky ones.

In early December of 2007, after traveling for only two months, she was able to board an old vessel that took her from the port of Tripoli to the coast of Malta.

She had arrived.

She had managed to defeat the monster.

She was in Europe.

CHAPTER 18

※

THREE WEEKS AFTER HODAN'S ARRIVAL, when everything seemed sad and gloomy without her, I received the news that changed my life forever and that I'd been waiting for since the day I was born: I would compete in the Beijing Olympics the following year.

When Xassan called me into his office to tell me, I couldn't believe my ears. As soon as he uttered the word "Olympics," my mind went blank. He kept talking, but I couldn't hear a word anymore.

"Samia, we think you can contribute a lot to our Olympic team and to our nation," he began.

"Thank you, Xassan," I replied.

"We value your efforts, your determination, and the will to win that you've been displaying."

"Thank you again, Xassan." It was the first time he'd summoned me to his office and said such things; I was trying to figure out where this was going.

"You won't place very high, Samia . . . but we thought you should use it as a trial run for the next Olympic Games, the ones in London in 2012 . . . to gain confidence. . . . So I'm asking if you feel up to going to China and running in those Olympics."

At that point the world was suspended. All my thoughts converged on a single image, a snapshot of calm and serenity: a wicker chair, the slanting light of the sun filtering through a window, only partly illuminating the dusty, earthen floor, a room, Aabe and Hooyo's, with me standing in front of Aabe promising him that, at seventeen, I would go to the Olympics.

And here came the tears. Two of them. The usual two.

Xassan thought they were tears of joy, and he made a joke that I only vaguely heard. But he was just half right. They came from deep inside, from my bitterness over the fact that Aabe was not there with me, that my sister wasn't there to share my joy, and that my best friend had fled many years ago along with his entire family.

The Olympic Committee had chosen me and Abdi Said Ibrahim, a boy of eighteen who in recent months had become my new friend and training partner. At first this had aroused a poignant yearning for Alì, but I quickly tempered and dismissed it.

Abdi and I trained every day.

But with Al-Shabaab having become more and more powerful, things had worsened. Sometimes we couldn't make it to the stadium because we were stopped by militants who insulted us or demanded money, accusing us of supporting Western countries. On those days we were forced to run on the street, amid smoking car tires and burning garbage in the squares, hoping not to come across other militiamen.

What's more, even though I was an athlete on the Olympic

team, I had to run covered. What I was doing, or in whose name, didn't matter to anyone. I had to respect the laws of the Koran and cover my head, torso, and limbs.

One morning Abdi was stopped and two Hawiye militiamen stole his shoes. "You'll run better that way," they told him. "Nigger. This way you'll run barefoot like a real African."

We always tried to ignore it. We were determined to train with what we had: no coach, no personal trainer, no doctor, not even food. Not the type of nourishing food suitable for an athlete, with the right amounts of calories, protein, vitamins, and minerals. At times just the food required to live.

Hooyo earned less and less, almost nothing by now, and every so often we were forced to eat only *angero*, a kind of crepe, made on the *burgico*.

Bread and water.

There was one thing I did have, and it had become one of my most important possessions: the stopwatch. With it I measured my times. Whatever else might happen, I was obsessed with my times. They had to improve. If I didn't see them improve from week to week, or if they worsened, I went into a deep funk that only Abdi could help me climb out of. In the end I started out again with even more energy.

We heard from Hodan frequently. She called us on Said's cell phone, or we texted for hours on the Internet. She had settled in Malta and was engaged to Omar, a Somali boy whom she had met during the Journey. He had helped her a lot, and it was partly thanks to him that she had made it. She had told me about Omar right away; I'd realized that she had fallen in love the first time she spoke his name.

In April we received some wonderful news, which at first seemed impossible to accept but which later filled me with joy.

Our little Hodan—who was my older sister, true, but was still, along with me, the youngest in the family—was pregnant.

She told us one morning, right after she took the test and confirmed it. She was ecstatic. She and Omar had been living together for some time in Malta, in housing provided by the government and humanitarian organizations. They had decided to start a family and move up north, maybe to Sweden, maybe to Finland, where assistance for war refugees was even greater.

Each time we texted, Hodan said she felt that it would be a girl and that she would be like me, with fast legs. She told me that already, at twenty weeks, the baby was kicking like crazy.

That's how I spent the four months before I was to leave for China: training, attending an occasional meeting at the Olympic Committee to learn how to improve Abdi's and my times, and chatting happily with Hodan.

Hooyo, however, was increasingly concerned.

Aabe's death and Hodan's departure had made any separation, even if only temporary, unbearable to her. Whenever one of us brought up the subject of the Olympics, Hooyo's eyes teared up. We told her she should be happy, that what was happening to me was very special, but by now she was able to see only the possible negative consequences of any event.

As might be expected, the news had spread quickly through the mutilated district of Bondere. The closer my departure came, the more people dropped by to see me and wish me well or bring me a small token of good luck. It happened almost every day before supper. These were all people with whom I'd grown up; they were my people, neighbors who had seen me born and develop into a young woman. People I loved and whose affection was for me a precious treasure.

"Have a safe trip, Samia, and bring honor to our country," old Asiya said in a trembling voice; the elderly woman had held me in her arms the day I was born. I considered her a kind of grandmother, given that two of my natural grandparents had died and the other two lived far away, in Jazeera. "Take this," she said as she handed me a cotton T-shirt. "I bought it at the market for your departure, to wish you good luck. I don't know if you'll want to wear it when you run. . . ."

"Of course, Grandma Asiya. Don't worry, I'll do my best. And I'll wear the T-shirt during training sessions," I told her.

"Samia, say hello to China for us and don't eat any of those strange little fried creatures," warned Taageere, the lifelong friend of Aabe and Aabe Yassin.

"Okay, Taageere, I'll only eat fresh fruits and rice," I reassured him.

And so it went.

Every day at least ten people came to give me their blessing.

When they paid me compliments, though, I tried to make light of it, to minimize it, saying that it was only a race, a competition like any other, nothing all that important.

But in my heart I couldn't minimize the importance of what I was doing.

I was little but I was also a warrior.

And the little warrior was ready, once again, to fight.

CHAPTER 19

❋

THE EVENING BEFORE I LEFT for China, Hodan called, saying she would soon give birth and was going to the hospital. Maybe that wasn't a coincidence either but a sign from destiny.

I felt bound to the little creature who was about to come into the world: a strong, vital bond, even though we were so far apart and I had never even seen Hodan's big belly. It was August 6, 2008.

That news was all it took to make me definitely sleepless. That night I didn't once close my eyes.

Just the idea of getting on an airplane filled me with anxiety; then too to go so far away, to the Orient, a place I'd barely heard of and that I knew only through stereotypes, scared me to death. I pictured people with yellow skin. And I'd never understood how they could see through those slits they had for eyes. Besides, they must be very swift; it would be like stepping into a crazed anthill. I was afraid. But most of all the race itself scared me. I had run many of them, but never, except for the one in Djibouti, a really important one. I didn't know what to expect.

What would the other girls be like?

I thought about real athletes, the women I considered my role models, and I felt totally inadequate. I didn't even have a coach.

I wondered what Abdi was thinking at that moment, in his bed. That morning at the track I saw that he was more agitated than I, or so it seemed. Would I be able to run? Or would I stumble at the first step and be left behind at the starting block, rolling on the ground like a floppy fish in front of TV cameras from around the world? Then I wondered: How many people would see my face? Xassan had told us that nearly a billion people would see us, in all the countries of the world.

A billion was a number I couldn't even imagine. When I thought of that many people, I thought about the stadium in Djibouti, the stands full of women, men, and children, jubilant and excited about the races. But my imagination stopped there. There must have been thirty thousand people, maybe. But a billion. What stadium could hold a billion people? These were questions that made my head spin. But then my thoughts would take a turn, and each time they would pause at the image of my infant niece who was about to be born and was already kicking in the belly to get out and run. And everything came back to the peaceful calm of familiar, known events.

It would all be over soon. China. The Olympics, that word that made me burst just thinking about it. It would all last no longer than a dream, and then I'd go back home, I would hug Hooyo and my brothers and sisters again, and I would resume running in my beloved, seedy field, as always.

The next morning three of us set off. Abdi and I and the vice president of the Somali Olympic Committee, Duran Farah.

What I had hoped for—that dawn would take away my fears—hadn't happened. No. The idea of landing in China charged me with adrenaline, but it was everything that came *before* then that filled me with terror.

The plane didn't just scare me. It put me in such a state of anxiety that I felt faint. Maybe partly because I hadn't eaten for days.

When they saw me at the Olympics Committee headquarters, Abdi, Xassan, and Duran Farah asked me if I was sick, if I had caught malaria. I was depleted. They forced me to drink sugar water and an energy drink. My stomach was so shrunken that I had to go to the bathroom to throw up that little bit of fluid.

At the airport the situation worsened rather than improving. I'd never been there before. For me, ever since I was born, airplanes had been dragons that plowed the sky, leaving behind endless white trails. I had never even thought that I might get on one. Let alone get on one at seventeen to go to Beijing.

We made it through the documents checkpoint with special permits that the Olympics Committee had managed to obtain for us with some difficulty. Neither I nor Abdi actually had a passport, since we'd been born during the war. Destined to live confined in our land, thanks to the mortars. Or, alternatively, to confront the Journey.

To our great surprise there was a small gathering of supporters to send us on our way: ten or fifteen in all, wearing the blue headband with the star of Somalia on their foreheads. From a distance we raised our arms; my heart was pounding nervously.

To get through the checkpoint I forced myself to try to appear as healthy as possible. As soon as we got past the officials, however, my legs were shaking so badly that I had to find something to lean on.

As we waited at the gate, I didn't move from the red velveteen chairs, while Abdi and Duran busied themselves at the Coke and coffee machines. When our flight was called, they looked at each other and nodded. To load me onto the plane, they forced me to swallow a sleeping pill dissolved in a plastic cup from the coffee machine.

I slept as only my infant niece, yet to be born, might sleep: the sleep of the just. Twelve hours straight, after collapsing soon after takeoff. Only the sight of the sea—which appeared unexpectedly below me as the plane cut through the clouds and which from above seemed like a miracle to be embraced—was able to hold off sleep for a few minutes. Then I succumbed to the power of the drug.

All in all, the flight was less difficult than I'd expected.

Upon arrival in Beijing I was beaming. Finally on the ground, everything was back to normal.

The airport was very modern, vast and striking. All glass and steel—you could see your reflection everywhere. The opposite of the one in Mogadishu, which by comparison looked like Taageere's bar, all wood and corrugated sheet metal. The glass doors opened by themselves, mirroring the image of three figures, two wearing blue track outfits and one in a dark suit, looking ill at ease amid all that technology: elevators, escalators, restaurants with shiny counters, Wi-Fi Internet hot spots, shops selling computers, cameras, and camcorders.

We were moving slowly in the midst of a sea of people who

by contrast were almost running; there were all nationalities speaking all languages. We felt inadequate faced with all that speed and modernity.

It was as if we'd come from another geological era. Would *everything* here be so fast? Even my opponents? And was I really so slow, deep down? Or was it just an impression, would I be like the others on the track? Maybe I carried my country's lethargy in my bones, and I would never reach their level.

Just outside Beijing's Capital International Airport we were assailed by an abundance of bodies and smells completely foreign from those I was used to. As if the air were both thicker and sweeter, more humid. As if someone, somewhere, were sprinkling confectioners' sugar around. It seemed like there was soot everywhere, and a pervasive stench of charcoal came from every corner.

"Hey, Abdi and Samia, move!" Duran yelled. The whole time we'd been standing motionless, looking around, he'd been on line for a taxi: Now he was standing next to a short, bald man in front of the open trunk of a yellow cab.

"Coming," we chorused, like two fish out of water. The same word in unison.

We hopped in the taxi, me and Abdi in back, and headed toward the center of the city.

Skyscrapers. Skyscrapers everywhere, so tall that from the car you couldn't see the tops of them. The scorching-hot sun reflected off the glass-and-steel facades, ricocheting in ways that seemed unnatural to us and that forced us to squint or lower our eyes. Again, as in the airplane, that powerful air-conditioning—it felt like being in a refrigerator.

Outside everything was dazzling and enormous. We passed

the aquarium, a giant cube of water and light. Abdi was speechless; he pointed to it and then he didn't speak for several whole minutes; he thought it was magic. In fact it looked that way. It was an immense glass structure that seemed full of water. But you couldn't see the glass, and the water seemed to stand on its own.

"But . . ." was all he said.

"Yes, dear Abdi, haven't you ever heard about it? Of course it's magic, like many things here in China. Haven't you ever heard of ancient Chinese magic?" I teased. Duran, up front, laughed. Abdi, however, was mesmerized, speechless.

After twenty minutes we arrived.

The hotel too was stunning. Nothing like the one in Djibouti.

Marble columns and floors, automatic doors.

The room was spacious and immaculate. There was a television set and a telephone. The softest bed I'd ever been in. Wall-to-wall carpeting. A wardrobe in which to put my few things. Towels of various sizes in the bathroom. Two amazing sinks, a huge counter with different kinds of creams, shampoos, and conditioners. On the marble floor, a rug in the colors of the Orient. And a bathtub.

We had the entire afternoon to ourselves. Duran had advised us only not to stray too far. But I didn't have the slightest intention of going out. There was a beautiful bathroom that was too good to waste wandering around the city.

I filled the tub. The contact with the hot water was a wonderful sensation. Like being all wrapped up in a big caress. The first bath of my life. The tension, the adrenaline, the concerns and fears were quickly drowned in that water, swallowed up in its warm embrace.

I think I must have stayed there soaking for at least two hours.

Then I got out and turned on the TV. Chinese channels, American channels. I could barely understand the English, even though I had studied it for years at school. I stretched out on the bed with the remote in my hand. I turned to the coverage of the Olympic Games on BBC and CNN. In exactly six days I too would be on that screen. The whole world would watch me run, would read my face, as I was now doing with the athletes who were competing.

"You can't lie," I said to myself. Everything you are will be seen. The whole world will see it. One billion people.

I got up from the bed and stood in front of the mirror that went from floor to ceiling alongside the TV table. I was extremely thin. I was truly a string bean. My legs were still spindly like those of a fawn; Aabe had been right when I was a little girl and he used to call me that. They hadn't filled out much since then.

I tried out two or three expressions up close to the mirror. Prostration at the end of the race. Poker-faced in front of the TV cameras before the start. A tense face during the race. Then I burst out laughing, all by myself, and lay down again.

I was on cloud nine.

That afternoon was wonderful. I had my whole life ahead of me, and my entire life would be full and glorious. I was a champion, and I had all the time in the world to prove it. I was a comet in a fabric studded with bright stars.

Six hours later we joined up again in the lobby to go out to dinner. I felt relaxed, and Abdi and Duran seemed so too.

We went out and ducked into the first restaurant we came to.

Abdi was hungry as a lion; he could have even eaten the table. He had to settle for the usual rice, though. He thought Chinese food was awful.

The opening ceremony of the Olympic Games was held two days later, on August 8. Being catapulted into a fantasy world inhabited by ten thousand other athletes from 204 nations, all parading in traditional dress, was the most thrilling event I had ever experienced. The delegations entered the Olympic stadium in alphabetical order by country. When it was our turn we were euphoric. The stadium had been going wild, still excited by the glittering ceremony: an endless succession of dazzling fireworks, light shows, music, dancing, and choreography that had involved thousands of performers including ballerinas, drummers, and opera singers. It was a celebration, a feast for the eye, ear, and soul. An incredible immersion in the warm, multihued heart that is universal love, whose different colors are nothing more than distinctive patches that strengthen it and allow the world to breathe.

Abdi, in front of us, carried the flag with pride. High, soaring, blue as the sky and sea. With the white star in the center pointing toward the firmament.

I, behind him, was in our traditional dress, with long braids attached to my hair for the occasion, and I felt as beautiful as I'd been only at Hodan's wedding.

We went around the arena waving to tens of thousands of people. They all loved us, and we loved all of them. Most of all, we loved our country.

That night, in bed, I told myself that life had already given me more than I deserved.

But I was mistaken.

Four days later, on August 12, Mannaar was born. I got the call from Hodan at the hotel that morning. She was bursting with joy. She said that Mannaar was healthy and beautiful, the same as me, that she looked exactly as I did when I was born. I couldn't wait to meet her. In my heart that morning I sensed that that child would be the joy of my life.

The day of my race, August 19, was extremely hot. The news that morning said that it would be one of the hottest days of the year. The heat didn't worry me; I was used to it. It was the high humidity: The heavy air left me breathless.

I woke up calm, with the urge to run. During those thirteen days Abdi and I had trained well, in a sports facility available to teams that required it. I was charged, full of energy.

Outside the stadium we could already begin to hear the roar of the spectators in the stands. It sounded like the buzzing drone of a giant fly, which rose as we entered the belly of the immense Olympic stadium.

I would be in the heat with one of my all-time legends, the Jamaican Veronica Campbell-Brown, one of the fastest athletes in the world. To be able to see her—instead of just hearing her name on Taageere's beat-up transistor radio—and to know that we'd be running in the same race was a feeling that made me dizzy.

We stayed out on the edge of the track for two whole hours to relish the sight of the other athletes who were competing. The more I watched the others, the more my adrenaline mounted. I couldn't wait to get on the track. The stands were huge, the crowd enormous. An infinity of colors, of different sounds, of voices and confusion, of banners in all the languages of the world. There seemed to be even more people than on the day of the opening ceremony.

Having the privilege of watching the performance as participants was a joy. Around us there were runners, javelin throwers, high jumpers, and pole-vaulters, some wearing the uniforms of their own countries, others ready to compete as independents. Every fifteen minutes a different national anthem rose, and meanwhile it all blended together like a giant rainbow. Abdi and I were sitting side by side on the ground at the edge of the track. Passing before us were blond German giants in black tracksuits, Italians in their blue uniforms, British in their white and blue T-shirts, Americans in red and blue, Canadians in red, Portuguese in green. It was an intoxicating mix of sounds and colors. Standing out above it all, whatever their garb, were the black athletes. Flawless, extremely tall, their sculpted muscles gleaming with ointments and adrenaline. All around, wherever you looked, there were TV cameras, photographers with lenses as long as the militants' rifles, journalists who swept down like hawks, microphones in hand, sporting badges from various newspapers.

When they came across me and Abdi, they looked at us to see who we were, then moved on. Not a word, not one question. Every now and then a smile of compassion or encouragement, when they realized by the colors of our outfits that we were Somalis.

We weren't stars.

Then we went back inside; the two-hundred-meter heats had been called.

Walking toward the tunnel leading into the stadium, I thought

I spotted a black British athlete out of the corner of my eye: red, white, and blue tracksuit, a familiar face. I turned around to get a better look and my heart skipped a beat.

Fifty meters away, in the middle of the green field, was Mo Farah. He was standing beside a sprinter who would shortly run the 4×100-meter relay. The latter was sitting on the ground stretching his muscles, and Mo was saying something to him. That delicate profile of his, like an antelope. Then they laughed together. I felt my knees suddenly grow weak, and at the same time I was tempted to run over to him, to tell him who I was, tell him about the worn-out photo I'd kept next to my mattress for nearly ten years. But I hesitated too long, because Duran took me by the elbow and led me inside. They were calling for us to enter the locker room.

"Come on. It's your turn, Samia," was all he said, rousing me from my daydream.

I had thirty minutes to myself: It was the period set aside to focus before the heat. I had to get Mo Farah out of my head and think only of the race.

I was alone. There was a massage table in the middle of the locker room. I lay down, closed my eyes, and pretended it was the grass at the stadium in Mogadishu. I tried to let go of any tension.

Suddenly, as if no more than a second had passed, I heard someone knocking gently at the door.

It was Duran. It was time.

Outside the locker room, as we began gathering in the hallway, I saw myself for what I was: different from the others. The wall of the tunnel leading out to the track was lined with mirrors:

With all of us together like that, our images were too conspicuous for me not to notice.

My legs, compared with those of the other women, looked like two dry sticks. They were straight, with no muscles. There were none of the bulges that I saw on the others' legs: I had no quadriceps, no calves. Also no deltoids, no trapezii, no biceps. The others looked like bodybuilders compared with me. Exaggerated legs and shoulders, calves extremely taut. I not only didn't have the machines to develop those muscles, but I didn't even have a coach. And I didn't have enough food, except for what Hooyo managed to get hold of. *Angero* and water. Or rice and boiled cabbage.

I was the shortest, the thinnest, and the youngest. It exposed me: That merciless mirror exposed me before the race.

In addition, the others wore beautiful, brightly colored outfits that matched the colors of their countries' flags. T-shirts and shorts in high-tech fabrics that clung to their powerful bodies. I had on my usual good-luck garb. A white T-shirt that Hooyo had washed the week before and that I had protectively left at the bottom of my bag. It still smelled of ash soap. My black tights that came below the knee. On my head, the white headband that Aabe had given me nearly ten years ago and that I had always brought with me to every race leading up to that day.

None of the other women looked at me. They were perfectly focused.

I should have been too, but it was all so different from what I was used to. I felt like I was in an unreal situation, in a dream. The TV cameras, the reporters, the stands overflowing with people, that continuous low roar that forced you to shout in someone's ear to make yourself heard, the athletes from all over the world, the scents of their deodorants, right there in front of me, under my nose. Veronica Campbell-Brown. Everything was simply incredible.

At that moment I remembered Mo Farah, my fellow countryman, perfectly at ease in the middle of the track, joking in English as he spurred on a white athlete. The opposite of me. By the time he was nine, he had already moved to England, so naturally it all seemed normal to him. He'd gone with his family. I was seventeen, and it was only the second time I had set foot outside my country. And the first time I'd traveled outside my continent. The first time I was among so many whites, so many Europeans, Americans, Chinese. I was indeed fortunate.

For a moment I saw Mo's face again, relaxed, calm, confident. I thought maybe he'd achieved an advantage that I could never hope to reach. Then I told myself that was silly; I too would get to where he was.

After five very long minutes we were called and went out, hit by deafening applause, all for Campbell-Brown. The humidity was very high; it made the tartan surface of the track shimmer in the distance.

It was the same track as always, the same length, but to me it seemed much longer. Twice as long, never ending.

I walked past Veronica Campbell-Brown: beautiful, flawless, imperious as a statue, fragrant as a diva. What perfume did she wear? All the power of those legs seemed to reside in their trim shape.

I was in the second lane, the innermost. To my left, the first lane was empty. On the right was Sheniqua Ferguson, the one everyone considered promising, originally from the Bahamas. In the fourth lane was the Canadian Adrienne Power, she too a strong runner.

In those interminable seconds I tried to do the one and only thing I had to do: focus my thoughts, which threatened to carry me away.

I crouched.

I placed my feet on the starting block, the right one and the left, pretending I was alone, that I was at the CONS stadium for a training session with Abdi. Or in the courtyard as a little girl, with Alì checking my feet on the block that Aabe had built from fruit crates.

It was just me and two hundred meters of tartan track in front of me.

Leaning on my knees, I placed my hands on the white starting line, fingers splayed, as Alì had taught me. One. Two. Three. Four. Five. Six. Seven. Eight. Nine. Ten. A number for each finger, to concentrate on the wait.

A thought of Aabe, as a good-luck charm.

Then, as if inside an infinite bubble, I waited only for the firing of the starting gun.

Boom. The pistol shot. A loud roar from the crowd.

The other runners took off like gazelles.

Incredibly swift, like dragonflies or hummingbirds.

They left their blocks before I even knew it.

I knew I would lose the race from the very first moment. With each stride the distance between me and the pack grew. An unbridgeable gap. My opponents sliced through the air; from behind they seemed like fillies flying in the wind.

I continued running. I held my head up and I pushed hard.

I was still at the curve when others were already across the finish line, catching their breath.

I ran the second half of the lap alone. But in those last fifty meters an unexpected thing happened.

Some of the spectators stood up and began clapping. In sync. They were urging me on, shouting my name, encouraging me. Like the day of my first win at the CONS stadium. Only this time the noise was deafening.

I would have preferred that they hadn't cheered. That they hadn't noticed I was so inferior.

I cut through the tape almost ten seconds later than the first runner, Veronica Campbell-Brown.

Ten seconds. An infinity.

I didn't feel shame, in any case. Only a strong sense of pride for my country. Instantaneous, as soon as I passed the finish line. People continued cheering as Campbell-Brown waved to the spectators and gave one interview after another, surrounded by a swarm of reporters.

In silence I completed a victory lap with Somalia's flag around my neck. Without fanfare, without anyone, perhaps, noticing. As I ran, my eyes searched for Mo Farah in the middle of the field. He wasn't there. I took a closer look all around. He was nowhere to be seen. He must have gone back inside, lost in the endless meanders of the Olympic stadium.

It was all over. It was really all over now.

Just as it had come, everything was already behind me.

I had finished last and yet, incredible as it was, after no more than ten minutes I too was engulfed by journalists from around the world. A seventeen-year-old girl, skinny as a rail, who comes from a war-torn country, without a track and without a coach, who fights as hard as she can and comes in last. A perfect story for Western sensibilities, I realized that day. I'd never had such a thought.

I didn't like it. I told the reporters that I would rather have had people applaud me because I came in first, not last.

But all I got in response was a smile of compassionate tenderness.

I'd show them.

In the locker room, under an ice-cold shower, I swore to myself that I would make it to the London Olympics of 2012, as prepared as Campbell-Brown.

With muscles where they should be and a heart as big and powerful as that of a bull.

In 2012 I would be the winner.

For my country and for me.

CHAPTER 20

※

WHEN I RETURNED HOME, life became even more difficult.

I received numerous letters, at home and at the Olympic Committee's headquarters, from Muslim women who had chosen me as a heroine, their ideal. Dozens, hundreds of letters. Each week more arrived. Some written in ink, some typed. Inadvertently I had become a legend for thousands of women who had seen me run without the veils on TVs throughout the world. Those letters from the United Arab Emirates, from Saudi Arabia, from Afghanistan and Iran contained a boundless passion. Hope. Dreams. Faith. In the eyes of the world I had been transformed into a symbol. And it had all happened without my seeking it in the least, without my even having thought of it.

For this same reason, however, going around on the streets had become even more difficult. Rumor had it that the Al-Shabaab fundamentalists hated me. They hated both me and Abdi, but I was a woman and therefore a double threat.

I was forced to wear a burka and cover my face in the country that I had represented, without veils, in front of cameras from around the world.

Luckily there was Hodan, who, from a distance, gave me joy.

We were now able to talk almost every night, and often I even brought Hooyo to Taageere's bar, where Hodan, who had meanwhile gotten a little webcam, would let us see Mannaar and hear her cooing via Skype. It was true what Hodan and Hooyo said: Mannaar and I were like two peas in a pod. She looked just like me when I was a baby. Hodan laughingly said that Mannaar wanted to become an athlete, just like her aunt.

Meanwhile, I continued training every day with Abdi. As the weeks went by, however, we realized that our performances would never improve. We needed support, a coach, a nutritious diet, a real track that wasn't riddled by bullets, proper equipment. Nothing like that existed in Mogadishu, and everything became more and more complicated with each passing day, each passing hour.

For a year I never stopped training with Abdi, every day of the week. A year. A whole year spent sweating to improve our times during every free minute we had. Yet they did not improve as they should have, with the speed that we would have expected, especially considering our age. We competed in races in Somalia or in Djibouti, and we even won, but it wasn't enough.

Something had to change.

At night in bed I prayed to the photo of Mo Farah to let me find a way. I wondered where he was now and what he was doing. We had tried to find a coach in Mogadishu, but no one seemed to be interested. In a country where there's shooting, no one cares about athletics. The warlords had no reason to sponsor us, and Al-Shabaab's men wanted us dead, just as they'd killed my father and Abdi's mother. Even the Olympic Committee lacked the clout and influence to attend to us.

We were lunatics nurturing an absurd folly. That's what we were. Lunatics whose dream was that of peace, the hope of living together as brothers.

In the end, however, my foolish nightly prayers to Mo Farah were answered, though in a way that was quite different from what I would have expected.

During those months I met an American journalist who often came to Mogadishu to cover sports in West African countries. Her name was Teresa. Teresa Krug.

She came to meet me at the stadium one morning; we did an interview and I immediately liked her. We essentially became friends. She often came back to see me, once a week, more or less.

We talked to the degree that I was able to. In this regard I took after Hooyo: Reticent and introverted, I didn't like answering questions about things that were too private. The family. Our poverty. My father. My friends. My siblings. My sister who made the Journey. I didn't feel comfortable with it; I wanted to talk only about running.

In the hours we spent together, Teresa kept telling me that I had talent and that I would have to leave Somalia. She claimed to know a coach in Addis Ababa, in Ethiopia.

One day, during one of our conversations, she asked me if I would like to go and meet him. She had already spoken to him about me. He had seen me race in Beijing and thought there was ample room for improvement in my running.

The more she kept telling me that, the more I knew that it

was the only thing to do. If I wanted to continue pursuing my dream, there was no other way. Here I would soon wither away like a wilted leaf.

What she held out, on the other hand, was what I wanted most of all: to have a coach, a normal place where I could train like any other athlete in the world, nutritious meals appropriate for my body, good running shoes, good T-shirts, good shorts. It would have been pure joy.

But I had made a promise to myself and to Aabe many years ago, and I had no intention of breaking it.

Teresa brought up the subject numerous times during those months, and I always said no. She would even help me leave, she said; she would try to facilitate the procedures for my papers.

In spite of this, I held firmly to my position: I would not leave Hooyo, my brothers and sisters, and my country for anything in the world.

One day I would manage to win the Olympics, and I would do it as a Somali and as a Muslim woman.

With my face uncovered and my eyes turned to the sky.

On camera I would tell the whole world what it meant to fight without means in order to achieve liberation.

CHAPTER 21

❋

THEN, shortly before Teresa was to leave Mogadishu to return to the United States, something unexpected happened.

I'd gone out after supper, covered by the burka, to return to the stadium. I still did that every now and then. I didn't go to train there but to feel the grass beneath my back, to stay and gaze at the stars awhile, to do what I would have liked to do at the beach but wasn't allowed to: relax, lose myself in the immensity of the sky, let my thoughts fly.

When I got back, Hooyo and my siblings had already gone to bed; the courtyard was silent and deserted. Only the lofty eucalyptus soared, oblivious to everything. Not a breath of air stirred; the tree's narrow leaves were motionless.

In the middle of the courtyard I noticed a small bundle resting on the ground and went over to it. It was a white *hijab* folded and tied up at the four corners to form a pouch. How strange. Could Hooyo have forgotten something outside? Yet it seemed to have been put there on purpose, waiting to be found. Right in the center of the big expanse of dusty white earth.

I opened it.

And it knocked the breath out of me.

Inside was a mountain of bills.

I tried to count them quickly. Maybe a million shillings. A ton of money. A family could live comfortably on it for two years. Eating meat twice a week, fish on Friday. It was a fortune.

Who could have . . . ?

Suddenly there was a thud from what had been Yassin and Alì's room. It had been years since it was used, though it seemed like millennia. For a time, while Aabe was still alive, he and Said had used it as a storeroom; then no one had gone near it. I hadn't set foot in it for ages. Since Alì and his family had left, I'd acted as if it no longer existed, as if it had never existed. Just the thought of all the hours that Alì and I had spent in there would have filled me with sadness.

Then I heard the noise again.

It must be a cat, or maybe a rat. Still, I had never heard any sounds coming from there before.

Slowly I approached the door. Nothing, not a sound. Then I opened it and stood in the doorway. It was very dark—the moonlight filtered in only faintly from the door—and the room smelled damp, musty, and dusty.

Gradually my eyes began to adjust to the dark.

The room was full of Aabe and Said's cartons, along with a few tools and piles of Hooyo's fruit crates, all stacked up. Everything had been heaped near the entrance, blocking the view toward the back, where I remembered Alì's family's mattresses were stored.

All of a sudden, I heard the same sound as before, but louder. It had to be a rat. I took a few steps forward.

Then I saw it.

A mattress had been moved against the back wall. On it, sitting cross-legged, was a shadowy figure.

I let out a stifled scream and leaped back, bumping into a large cardboard box and losing my balance. I was on the ground. I was making an abrupt move to get up when a voice spoke.

"Samia."

It was a man, maybe a boy, a male in any case, but the voice told me nothing else.

"Samia, it's me. Don't you recognize me?"

I squinted and took a closer look at the shadow. He had long hair and an unkempt thicket of beard on his chin and cheeks.

A shiver of cold terror ran down my spine.

I didn't breathe.

"It's Alì."

I moved nearer to him. Could that bearded man really be Alì? Was that lined, sunken, stricken face his?

I took another step, bumping the mattress with my foot. The eyes were those of my best friend, but they were hidden behind a hardened shell.

I knelt down on the mattress and right away, up close like that, I had the urge to touch him.

At first he drew back, but then he yielded.

We hugged each other tighter than we'd ever done before. On that dusty mattress in a room full of cobwebs and dampness.

"You've come back?" I asked. I recalled that night so many years ago, when Aabe had given me a pair of sneakers and I had gone into that same room to show them to my friend. He had been lying on the mattress, hiding his head under his arm. He had been little then. A child.

"I'm leaving," he replied. His voice was unfamiliar. Only his small, close-set eyes and flat nose were as I remembered. The lips were surrounded by the black beard; I couldn't see them clearly.

"What do you mean you're leaving? You just got back!"

"I've stayed too long. We weren't supposed to meet." His voice was harsh.

"Why did you come home?"

"To leave you the *hijab*. . . ."

A pause.

Then he started sobbing and told me everything.

He had joined Al-Shabaab many years ago, shortly after his father, Yassin, had made the decision to leave Bondere.

His brother Nassir had already been recruited, having gone along with his friend Ahmed. For Aabe Yassin it had been a terrible blow, and he had thrown Nassir out of the house. He had feared that Alì would end up pursuing the same path, following his older brother. So they had moved far away to the south, to the small town of Jazeera, where Yassin and Aabe had been born and raised. There his father had hoped to keep him away from the extremists. But he had been mistaken, because Ahmed and Nassir had introduced Alì to the administrative committee of Al-Shabaab even before the family left. That's why Ahmed had been looking for Alì that afternoon.

It had been a difficult decision for him: Should he follow his brother or listen to his father? In the end he had given in. Shortly after the move to Jazeera, he'd left Yassin's house and joined Nassir.

For the first time in his life he'd felt he was being treated like he was worth something; he'd gone to school, he'd learned to write, he had a decent place to live, a bathroom, three meals a day.

"Remember when I was little and couldn't even read?" he asked me with that hard-edged voice. "I only learned how later, thanks to you and your running and those old manuals from the library."

My voice was all choked up; I couldn't answer. All I could do was nod my head as I stroked his arm.

"Since the day I followed my brother, I got everything. What I'd never had, what I'd never been."

I squeezed his hand and gestured for him to go on.

Yassin had renounced him and his brother and turned his back on them, but as a result of that they found themselves free to have the life they would never have been able to afford. An education, clean clothes, full bellies.

Alì immediately excelled in Koranic studies, in the use of weapons, and in military strategy. He quickly outshined Nassir and even Ahmed, who had meanwhile been sent to a training camp near the Lamu Archipelago, off the northern coast of Kenya. At a very young age Alì had earned the trust of Ayro himself, the head of Al-Shabaab.

At that point Alì stopped; he could no longer continue.

I begged him to go on; there was a coldness and emptiness in his eyes that scared me, but those sobs were pleading to be heard, to be forgiven.

"Go on, Alì. I'm here," I told him, swallowing the lump in my own throat and caressing his face.

"I had to do a bad thing. . . . I had to do something that I would never . . ." Again he burst into tears that he'd been holding back. Mucus was running out of his pinched nostrils; he looked like the little boy I'd always known. I held his hands tightly and told him not to worry.

In the meantime my eyes had adjusted to the darkness, and I could now better make out his features, the good fabric of his clothes.

Around us there was only silence and a strong musty smell.

Alì took a breath, wiped away his tears, and continued.

The fundamentalists knew me and my sister Hodan; they called us "the two little subversives." They also knew our father, who had never been willing to bend to the Islamic warlords. They knew that Alì and I had grown up together in the same house. After my win in Hargeysa, Ayro had gotten it into his head to teach me a lesson that would make me get over the urge to run.

They had to get rid of Aabe.

And so Ayro had gone to Alì and asked him to point Aabe out to the man who was to shoot him.

He'd had no choice. It was the cruelest, most heartless thing for him, as if he'd been asked to kill his own father. Yet if he hadn't agreed to do it, many more people would have been blown up along with the intended target. With the help of someone who knew Aabe, however, they could just gun him down.

So that morning at the Bakara market Alì had hidden among the crowd and stayed close to Aabe for a while. Close enough to smell his scent, which he remembered perfectly. The scent of his clothes, which for years had been the same as his own, since Hooyo did the wash for Alì's family as well.

Then Alì's eyes turned cold and he stopped talking.

I was petrified, turned to stone. The words had entered my ears, but it was as if they didn't want to go all the way to my brain and had stopped there, waiting for me to shake my head and pitch them out. I don't know what I did, maybe nothing. Maybe I shouted or cried. I don't know. I don't know how much time went by either.

Then Alì said that the money was everything he had earned during those years, and he wanted us to have it. With a bitter smile he said that in the end he was like his father, who had wanted to compensate Aabe with money after Aabe had been wounded in his place. He knew it could not repay us, but it was the only thing he could do.

"I've repented, Samia. I'm out of Al-Shabaab now."

I didn't open my mouth.

"If you can, forgive me . . . *abaayo* . . ."

Silence.

Then, slowly, he stood up.

Before turning to go, he laid a hand briefly on my shoulder.

When he was almost at the door, he added: "You'll see, you'll make it to the London Olympics too."

They were the last words I heard him say.

Then he was gone.

I turned around.

I was left with the image of his broad black back projected against the moonlight.

I don't know how long I sat there like that. Motionless, with tears streaming down my face and a thousand questions like pinpricks in my head. I was confused. What Alì had told me, something he must have repeated to himself many times in the solitude of his bed, was devastating.

How could he have? How could he have forgotten all the times

Aabe had held him in his arms and spoon-fed him as a child while his father, Yassin, looked after the other boys? How could he fail to recall the countless occasions when Hooyo had been a mother to him, washing and dressing him, cooking for him? How could he?

These and a million other questions raced through my mind. But I'm certain that the moment his back stood out in the moonlight was the moment I made the decision to leave.

In one instant, in that one image, my whole world fell to pieces forever. If my country had been able to make a monster out of the boy who had always been a brother to me, my soul mate, if it had turned him into my father's killer, then that meant I was worth nothing to my country.

Aabe was Somalia. But Somalia was now dead, killed by a brother.

I was wasting my time. I had already thrown away enough years and talent in a place that didn't want me. And that never missed an opportunity to remind me of it, subjecting me daily to shame and sweat and forcing me to endure the worst humiliations on the street wherever I went.

I had been exhausted for years, but I'd never wanted to admit it.

Hodan had been right.

I would do as she'd done.

I would do as Mo Farah had done.

The next morning I asked Said to lend me his cell phone. I called Teresa in America and told her that I would go with her. Hooyo would understand; my brothers and sisters would accept it.

"I've made up my mind. I'm going with you to Addis Ababa," I told her.

CHAPTER 22

HODAN WAS HAPPY about my decision, saying that I had finally found the courage to leave that country and wholeheartedly follow my dream. In the meantime, she and her husband, Omar, and Mannaar had moved to Helsinki, where the government would soon provide them with a house and a monthly allowance.

Mannaar was my joy. At almost a year and a half she was still identical to how I had been at her age. Sassy, with animated eyes, a tall, skinny beanpole. Hodan would do everything she could to enroll her in an athletics class once she turned two, which was actually common practice up there.

I didn't want even one shilling of Ali's money. Together Hooyo and I decided that she would keep half and the other half would go to Hodan for Mannaar. Not a single day should be wasted. We would know soon enough if she really had talent, but meanwhile she would be given the best possible start, and maybe she would get to her first race with the body of Veronica Campbell-Brown. She would win more races than me, and earlier than I had.

The endless wait for the documents required to leave the country was marked by an infinite tenderness that I had begun to feel for everything that was closest to me, for my brothers and sisters, for Hooyo, and for all my usual places. One day I even burst into tears with Abdi during a break in our training session: Sitting in the middle of the field, I told him that I would miss him and the CONS stadium so much.

"How can you miss a track full of bullet holes?" he asked me as he retied his shoelaces and got ready to start running again. True. Yet I knew that I would miss everything, and I lived each hour trying to absorb as many memories as possible, soaking up details that would be precious to me.

Another afternoon the same thing happened to me at Taageere's bar when he insisted that I drink a *shaat* with him. "Soon you will go," he said. And I burst into tears again. "Don't cry, little champion," kind old Taageere continued as he poured a little milk in the tea; his face was furrowed with wrinkles so deep that it looked like one of those masks representing Iblis, the devil. Except that he had gentle eyes turned down in an expression of constant compassion. "When you get there, you will quickly forget us. And when you come back, you'll be so famous that you won't even have time to come and say hello," he said as he finished stirring the *shaat*. "If you don't, I swear I will come to your house and make you tell me everything, one way or another." I ended up crying on his shoulder, releasing some of the anxiety that clenched my stomach. He hugged me, then considerately changed the subject, speaking softly as always.

It took me six months to leave. That's how long was needed to arrange for my expatriation papers.

Teresa had overseen the whole process from afar, and when the time came she returned to Mogadishu. She had become my guide and mentor. I had decided to put myself in her hands. Teresa was only twenty-six years old, but she already had a lot of experience, had lived in many countries, and knew her way around. I had finally decided to stop resisting and trust her. She was my passport to freedom.

The day I said good-bye to Hooyo and my brothers and sisters was very sad. Unlike Hodan, who had surprised us all with her departure, my leave-taking went on for a whole day, starting the afternoon before. I would be back before long, I kept saying; Ethiopia wasn't far away. As soon as I started winning more international competitions, I would have enough money to come and go whenever I wanted.

I took only the essentials with me: almost nothing, as usual. My racing outfit. The tracksuit. A few shillings. Aabe's headband and the photo of Mo Farah, which I'd taken off the wall after ten years. By now the page was tattered. It was no longer paper; it was an image and a dream printed on butterfly wings. The two medals from Hargeysa were left there, hanging from a nail now rusted by dampness. As she'd done with Hodan, Hooyo gave me a handkerchief with one of the shells that Aabe had given her many years ago. She wanted me to carry it with me always: It was her protection. She folded the cloth into a band and tied it tightly to my wrist with two knots. Hidden between the folds, the tiny shell couldn't even be seen.

"That way you'll carry your beloved sea with you," she told me. "The entire sea in this seashell."

Teresa had to wait awhile for me in the taxi before I could

tear myself away from Hooyo. I couldn't help it; I just couldn't leave her. Finally I clenched my fists, gave her one last kiss, and went to confront my new destiny like a soldier or a warrior going off to battle.

We would travel by plane and would land, after a two-hour flight, at two in the afternoon.

It was the second time I had been taken to the airport by car, and this time my frame of mind was very different. I didn't even need a sleeping pill for the flight. I was so sad that I wasn't afraid of anything. Fear is a luxury afforded by happiness.

In the few hours since I'd obtained my papers, everything in my life had changed. In what seemed like just moments, as if I'd been catapulted through time, I was somewhere else, in another world, ready for a new start.

During the trip Teresa and I talked nonstop. Teresa kept telling me to focus on what was to come and forget about all the things that had slowed my career. It would take some effort, but I could do it. If I had made it to the Olympics on my own two legs, I'd be able to do that too.

CHAPTER 23

✳

WAITING FOR US at the airport in Addis Ababa was Eshetu
Tura himself.

He had been an athlete in his youth and now he trained tal-
ented runners. He would be my coach. He was tall and lean, with
muscular shoulders that seemed at odds with his graying hair and
a face that was no longer youthful. He wasn't as I had imagined;
in my head I'd pictured him younger, but he was very elegant,
both in the way he dressed and in his manner.

His consideration and courtesy immediately inspired my trust.

"Welcome to our city, Samia," he said in English as he held
out his hand.

"Thank you very much, er . . ." I paused as I shook his hand.
I didn't know what to call him, whether by his first or last name.

"Coach. You can just call me coach for now." He broke into a
big smile that put me at ease. Then he motioned to the bag, which
I had set on the ground, as if to say that he would carry it. And
so he did. Teresa was traveling with an overnight case; she would

stay only a couple of days. I let Eshetu put my bag over his shoulder.

"Let's go now. There's a taxi waiting for us."

The city was much bigger than Mogadishu and also much more modern. The buildings were intact, the plaster wasn't peeling, and the balconies weren't falling down; to me it seemed like a miracle. That's why I rolled down the window and enjoyed the crisp, clean breeze coming from outside. I needed the fresh air on my face to realize that it was all different. Everything was suffused with a distinct smell, even though the terrain was similar to what I was used to.

"The air here is scented," I said to Teresa, who was sitting in the back with me.

"It's not scented; it's normal, Samia. It's just that you don't smell the stench of gunpowder." I had never thought about it. The smell of gunpowder had been born before I was, spawned by my older sister, the war, and I had never considered it anything but the normal smell of air. Now I was breathing air as it should be, and the breeze was already transforming me.

The taxi left me and Teresa at a hotel, where we would stay for a few days, until I was settled in my new quarters. We said good-bye to Eshetu and arranged to meet in two days.

When I left the hotel, I would live in a small apartment in an area near the sports field, along with eleven other Somali and Ethiopian girls. Teresa had been the one to find the place, thanks to a journalist friend who often came to Addis Ababa. It would be my new home. Of course, there wouldn't be a lot of room, but at least it was cheap; I couldn't afford more than that.

Two days later Teresa left. A new laceration. With her departure the last tie that bound me to my city was broken. We had become friends and had had time to get attached to each other. Now I was alone again. Once again someone dear to me had left me.

We said good-bye like sisters. "See you soon, *abaayo*," I said at the door of the hotel room that I would leave that same day.

"See you soon, Samia. Maybe when you come to the U.S. for a big race," she replied with tears in her eyes before closing the door.

From that day on I would be alone.

Alone with my desire to run.

The apartment had only two bedrooms, plus a kitchen and a bathroom. It was small, and there were twelve of us, but I had never known such conveniences.

From the moment we met, I quickly made friends with the two Ethiopian girls, Amina and Yenee. They were my age and, like the other nine girls, worked on a farm just outside Addis Ababa. All of them were field hands hired by the day. The house we lived in belonged to the landowner.

They worked in two shifts, morning and afternoon. Amina and Yenee usually did the afternoon shift, so we often cooked together. The kitchen was really tiny, its floor and walls completely covered with the same greenish blue tiles. There was a gas stove with an oven. Beside it were a sink, a cabinet for dishes and glasses, and a refrigerator—the first one I'd ever had. Amina and Yenee let me taste their traditional Ethiopian dishes, and I had them try Somali cooking. We made ourselves understood by gestures, but we soon invented a language of our own, a mixture of Somali, Ethiopian, and English.

The apartment was on the top floor of a four-story building that wasn't bad looking, its walls covered with red plaster. Down below there was even a small garden where dogs did their business. We slept six to a room, on six mattresses lined up beside one another. Since I was the last to arrive, mine was farthest from the door. To get to it I had to climb over the other girls.

At the end of the day the girls were very tired; working in the fields was exhausting. Some of them took a dislike to me from the beginning, especially two Somalis from the outskirts of Mogadishu, who saw me as a princess who had nothing better to do in life than run.

One night before going to bed, when we were together in the small kitchen, Amina, tired of the malicious remarks made by those two, came out with the fact that I had gone to the Olympics, that I had run for their country.

"I don't give a shit about where she was before she came here," one of the two Somalis retorted; she was very beautiful and could have been a model. "She's here just like we are now. You can tell things aren't going very well for her either."

She had a point.

"Besides, she didn't even win," the other one added; she was tall and heavyset, her eyes perpetually apathetic, as if everything were a bore. "She could have made us look better." She too had a point.

Nevertheless, during those first weeks I breathed the scent of freedom, of the absence of gunpowder. I had friends and I could go around without fear of someone shooting me. I could go to the market, which was much smaller than the Bakara market but still full of goods and people; I could shop there or in some small supermarket, go home, and cook.

Normal things that to me, however, seemed incredible. I felt full of energy; every event filled me with enthusiasm.

Soon enough, though, I realized that it wouldn't be as easy as I had thought. I was there to run. I would have done so from day one, but at first Eshetu told me that it wasn't yet possible. I had to be patient and wait, maybe two weeks. Things still weren't ready for me, but they would be soon.

I felt like a filly with no bridle and no saddle. I needed to lengthen my stride, keep my muscles moving.

The days passed and my impatience grew. I did exercises at home when the others weren't there, but most of all I wanted to run.

Before long I even started working in the afternoon: To support myself I helped the landlady, the landowner's wife, sew lace on clothes. I went to her apartment, which was next door to ours on the same floor, and spent four hours with her and thirty other women sewing all types of different lace onto thousands of women's garments. The kind that Muslim women wear under the veils, all transparency and sensuality. That was her job, and I helped her, sitting on the floor in a large room with a multitude of girls. We sat there in silence, retracing those secret intrigues, weaving the threads of future forbidden pleasures. No one said a word. The landlady turned on the radio and we worked to the sound of traditional Ethiopian music. She paid me very little, but it was still something. Besides, maybe the Somali girl was right: I couldn't go to work in the fields; I had to conserve my body for the race.

In fact, as I worked, all I thought about was when I would start running again.

Then the truth came out.

I could not use the track until documents arrived from Somalia confirming the fact that I was an Olympic Committee athlete in political asylum in another country.

Six weeks had already gone by. A month and a half without running. I tried to make Eshetu understand that it was suicide, that I should run regardless, because those documents could take months, if not years, to come and in the meantime I was in danger of forgetting what a tartan track was like. I tried to make him see that things in Somalia were worse than he imagined. That it might be years before those documents arrived. I tried in every way I could to persuade him to let me train with his other athletes. But there was no way.

"You cannot, Samia. I am sorry. You have to get it through your head," he repeated in his polite voice each time I pounced on him. "You cannot, Samia."

I kept insisting: It couldn't end like this; it was absurd that I should have to wait months before I could start training. "But I ran in the Olympics! I'm a famous athlete! Do you know how many women have written to me?" I burst out once.

Nothing for it; he didn't bite. The answer was always the same.

"You cannot."

I went there every day, each time hoping it would be the right time. One afternoon I skipped the lace work and charged into his office in tears: I was willing to do anything to get started. Eshetu was furious; he said I couldn't suddenly show up there. I wasn't yet authorized to use the facility, and if they found me it would be even worse. I kept insisting but it was no use. Then, finally, when I had decided to give up and was about to hang my head and leave, he said: "There may be a solution, however. It's the only way." Head tilted, he looked at me through the eyeglasses he used for reading.

I leaped up from the chair across the desk from him. "I'm willing to do anything," I cried.

"You can run at night. When the other athletes have left the field."

Still at night. Still alone. Even more alone.

It couldn't be further from what I had hoped for when I decided to leave.

I would be in hiding again.

Only this time it was even worse. I was no longer in my country. I was a foreigner without papers, without a passport. Nothing official to attest to my identity and where I came from. That was another thing that being Somali meant: not being able to be seen in someone else's country.

"You have to get it through your head that for some people here you're a *tahrib*, an illegal immigrant, Samia. You have to be careful what you do," Eshetu continued. "You can't display yourself too much."

From a "little subversive," as Alì had said they'd called me, I had become a *tahrib*, a clandestine figure.

Was that what fate had in store for me? A return to the days when I went to the CONS stadium at night and trained for hours in silence?

But there was no alternative if I wanted to run.

"Okay. I'll train at night when the others have gone."

And that was it. Each day I met Eshetu at the entrance to the field and watched the others leave, tired and happy after a day of training. Then, head down, I entered the locker room, which still smelled of their sweat and their shower gels.

As the sun set and the moon rose, I made my furtive entrance onto the track.

The first run was a liberation and a joy for the legs, which had been still for too long. Finally the muscles were able to function again, to let their power explode. But nothing could shake the thought that I was some kind of undesirable little mouse.

Eshetu was there the first few days, watching me run and correcting me, assigning me targeted exercises.

It was great to have a professional coach look after me for the first time. I felt that was the only way I could grow as an athlete. He would be able to mold me into the form of a perfect runner.

"You waste too much energy, Samia," he told me.

"You lift your heels too high."

"You move your arms too much. Hold them still!"

"Don't roll your shoulders at every stride, Samia! How many times must I tell you? Start over!"

"Your eyes should always be fixed on the finish line. Don't look around; you're wasting time!"

"Those hands, Samia! Keep them still! Still! Every unnecessary movement means the loss of a few tenths!"

"You have no quads, Samia. I'm sorry. You need to develop some muscles first of all. Work out on the machines. You can't move a train on wagon wheels!"

"Breathe, breathe, breathe! You have to work on the breath and on the muscles. How do you expect to run otherwise?"

"Reps and the machines, Samia. Remember that. Reps and the machines. For six months, every day: two hours of reps and an hour and a half on the machines!"

Two-hundred-fifty-meter sprints at maximum power every day. And forty-five minutes on the weight machines before and after each workout.

Nothing else for weeks and weeks.

For five months.

Every week I called home, to Said's phone, and told them that everything was perfect. That I lived in a beautiful apartment and that I was training with a coach who was bringing out the best in me.

They were all happy for me. Hooyo cried each time and was relieved to hear my voice. For me it was the only way I could go to bed at peace.

At the beginning Eshetu stayed for the entire workout. Then he left me alone to complete the sprints and work out on the machines. Finally he didn't even wait anymore: I knew what I had to do. He went home to eat with his family. Only the grounds-keeper, old Bekele, was left with me. Every so often he emerged from his booth and applauded me, cheering me on. I could make out his minute shadow, its silhouette illuminated by the moon behind him.

I was glad to be gaining strength, and I was pleased with the work that Eshetu was making me do. It was just that I had a need to compete, to measure myself against the others. A need that was becoming increasingly urgent. Was all that effort leading to results? I craved what I liked best about running: competing. Pushing myself to the extreme. Winning.

During those months in Addis Ababa I realized that winning

was an irreplaceable fuel, that only victory could give me the energy to continue. But that wasn't possible there. To compete I needed the light of day, not the shadows of night. I needed other athletes.

Instead there I was again, alone, at night, on a field. Once more under the light of the moon.

The more months passed, the greater the certainty that the documents from Somalia would never come. Nor, with them, the possibility that Eshetu might treat me like the others, signing me up for competitions, letting me compete, putting me to the test.

Every so often I went to the field before the end of the training sessions and watched the others run from outside the wire mesh fence, for fear that Eshetu might see me and get angry. If they were to catch me at the field, he said, if they were to do an inspection and find me there, I would likely not be able to use it anymore, not even at night. So I went a little early and watched them run from outside. I stood there gripping the green diamond-patterned wire mesh and observed them. Sometimes I hid behind a hedge near an electricity meter, and from there I spied on them, the way you spy on those kissed by fate, by good fortune.

I forgot about the races I had won, about the Beijing Olympics, all of it. I became an amateur dreaming about racing. While the others seemed unreachable. They were perfect. Incredibly swift. It was like being in front of the TV. Power, precision, dedication, drive. It was all there in their movements.

They were everything I might never be able to be. I remained a *tahrib*, running alone.

But in truth there was only one thing I wanted, and that was to win.

Little by little during those months, without even being aware of it, I began to entertain the desire to leave that place as well. I realized that occasionally, talking with Amina and Yenee, I would speak about Addis Ababa and our house as if they were already part of the past, as though I felt the need to start preserving their memory. Even though I was there.

I lived the last few months in a kind of melancholy countdown toward the future. The more I began to feel uncertain about what was to come, the more I tried to stamp those places and sensations in my memory. As in Mogadishu six months earlier. I had a premonition that those memories would accompany me on a Journey that I couldn't decide to face but that I increasingly felt was crucial.

I said things like "Someday I'm going to miss your cooking and all the commotion you make before you go to bed." They looked at me and didn't understand. They thought I was homesick for my house and for Hooyo and that that was why I was sad every now and then.

Though I realized it only later, the truth is that those six months flew by and gave breath to the desire to leave behind the condition of *tahrib* for good.

Slowly, day by day, the desire to join Hodan in Finland took shape, the urge to find a competent coach in a place where I wasn't an illegal and could do everything like a normal person, like any other girl.

More than anything else I wanted to feel normal, ordinary. I had to leave there. It was the only way to qualify for the London Olympics and try to win them. I understood that now.

At ten o'clock one morning, after planning everything in

secret, without saying a word to anyone, not even to Eshetu or to Amina and Yenee, I tossed my few belongings in my bag and left.

On the table I left the money for the week's rent and a note: *Dear Yenee and Amina, I'll miss you. Good luck, Samia.*

I left on foot, alone. In my pocket, the money I'd earned working during those six months.

Like Hodan, I would get to Europe.

I would face the Journey.

It was July 15, 2011. I had just turned twenty and still had one more year to qualify for the Olympics.

I would make it, there was no doubt.

In a short time I'd be gone from there.

Safe at last.

Safe.

CHAPTER 24

❋

KNOWING WHERE TO FIND the human traffickers was easy. All the Somalis in Addis Ababa knew it, and in recent weeks I had asked the right questions. Sooner or later every Somali living in Ethiopia would turn to them in order to get to Sudan. And from there to Libya. And then finally to Italy.

It wasn't difficult to track down Asnake.

As a cover, Asnake worked at the Addis Ababa market. I would have to pay the equivalent of seven hundred American dollars in reali, the Ethiopian currency. He or one of his friends would take me to Khartoum, in Sudan. I didn't have much more money, but I had no choice, and I didn't want to wait any longer. So I went to Asnake and he told me to be patient, that I couldn't leave right away; they would let me know when my day came.

I waited those last ten days trying to stay calm and not let on to Amina and Yenee; I didn't want any questions; I didn't want to explain myself.

Then one morning around ten o'clock Asnake sent a boy to the house to summon me.

We would leave three hours later. The first time I'd met Asnake he had warned me that I would have no time to prepare, that when the time came, it came, and I would have to leave immediately. But I really didn't need to prepare; I had been waiting for that moment for days now.

So I tossed my few belongings in my bag, rewound Hooyo's handkerchief with the shell around my wrist, took a bottle of water, left a note for Amina and Yenee, and left.

As I resolutely performed those small acts, I had no idea what I was committing myself to.

The meeting place was a garage that was used to store motorcycles or bicycles. When I arrived, almost everyone was already there waiting. All together there were a lot of us; I had always thought it would be just me, or at least just a few of us. Instead I counted seventy-two of us.

We were left there for an hour, not knowing what to do, inside that garage with the rolling shutter pulled down. Crammed into a tiny space. With each passing minute I wondered what would happen. I hugged the bag tightly under my arm. It was my past, my history: Right away I felt the need to make contact with something familiar, a memory. Surrounded by so many people you're likely to lose yourself, to give up; I realized that right away. There were mothers with children, a lot of women, and even some elderly people. The acrid smell of gasoline and burned oil quickly tainted what little oxygen there was; in addition, the sweating bodies soon gave off a nauseating odor. We were close together, packed so tightly that the skin of our arms touched. Under the veils we were drenched; the men had drops of perspiration on their faces. And so we waited. No one knew exactly for what.

After an hour the children began crying. That senseless waiting was getting on our nerves. We would have to wait longer. After another hour the shutter was rolled up and a Land Rover arrived with six men.

When I realized that all seventy-two of us were expected to crowd into the open bed of the jeep, my legs buckled and I had to grab hold of the woman standing beside me. Some of the others were desperate; a few seemed to know it all.

With no time to think, we were ordered to pile everything we had in a corner. Everything. They would see to our bags later. Each of us was allowed only one small plastic bag. One of the traffickers distributed them. Nobody wanted to be separated from his baggage: Inside was all that remained of our lives. Like premature butterflies, we didn't want to leave our cocoons. I thought about the headband, the newspaper clipping; I touched the shell at my wrist. Then, like a lightbulb going off, came the thought of returning, running back to the house, tearing up the note on the table and acting like nothing had happened. Sooner or later the documents would come; I just had to hang on.

The traffickers came forward to seize the bags of those up ahead who didn't want to let go of them. A few people tried to protest; the answer was that if they didn't like it, they could stay there.

Did I really want to stay in Addis Ababa? For how long? My whole life? For how long would I have to run by moonlight, like a cockroach? I opened my bag and took out Aabe's headband, the photo of Mo Farah, a *qamar,* and a *garbasar,* and I left all the rest in the corner.

Immediately my bag was buried under a thousand others.

In silence the six men set out two benches in the center of the jeep's bed, so as to form four rows of seats. It seemed impossible that we could all squeeze in. But slowly, with a surgical precision that suggested the skill of certain craftsmen, they fit us in like pieces of a puzzle.

We had to keep our knees open to make room for a stranger's leg between them.

I was so wedged in that I was barely able to breathe. Again I had the urge to get out of there. Then a baby started wailing in my ear, and I came to my senses.

I tried to remember why I was there. I had to keep going.

The trip was to last three days; it was critical that we bring nothing with us but the plastic bag: The jeep would be our living space for seventy-two hours, they told us. We couldn't even bring water. They had jerricans for all of us.

They did another round of inspection and confiscated a few things from those who thought they were being smart.

After half an hour packed in like sardines, our breath already caught in our throats, we finally left. With the driver and his backup in the cab and seventy-two of us in the bed. The other four men stayed behind to scoop up the baggage.

We knew it once we were on our way: We were leaving our bags behind forever. Just as I was leaving behind forever my life as it had been up till then. I realized it right from the start, crushed between those unfamiliar bodies. Nothing would ever be the same. I was leaving behind Africa, my family, my land. My cocoon, big or small, good or bad though it might be. All that was left of my past was crammed inside a white plastic bag.

Was that all my life was worth up to that point? My heart told me otherwise, even as it pounded in my chest.

I held back tears, biting my lip hard. I closed my eyes in the midst of all those arms, shoulders, elbows, and I prayed to Aabe and to Allah. That they would let me find the way.

My way.

The first stretch was through the city. During those twenty minutes driving through Addis Ababa, I felt shame. A shame not divided by seventy-two but multiplied by seventy-two. I felt like a nonentity. We stopped at a traffic light, the one that led onto the national boulevard. The eyes that watched us were filled with a mixture of pity and suspicion.

Why had we let ourselves be reduced to that, they wondered.

Then we finally left the city and took the great desert highway, as everyone calls it: the big road leading to the north. At each jolt I thought my liver would burst, or my spleen, because of the dozens of elbows poking me on all sides. The city's asphalt had given way to the usual dirt road, which, exposed to the rain and brutal sunlight, was studded with deep potholes.

The road was absolutely straight, and we kept up a steady speed of about eighty kilometers an hour, but after a while some people began to feel sick in those conditions. I was having trouble breathing; every now and then I felt faint and had to make a superhuman effort, prying aside the others, to sit up a little and find some fresh air. I kept thinking of the wind, which Alì used to tell me to ride. Stretches of green swept by wind and graced by yellow butterflies. That's the image I held in my mind. That's what filled my eyes. That's what I forced myself to picture, so as not to think.

At first no one had the courage to complain; it was more like a subdued moaning. Then the lament became louder until it spewed into vomiting.

Since we couldn't move our arms, the vomit ended up on everyone around us. We couldn't shield ourselves; we were windows open to the world and all types of weather.

We passed through two villages with not many inhabitants.

Those small communities had been preceded by huge, colorful billboards: a pair of lions with flowing manes and underneath the name of a travel agency advertising safaris: a big off-road vehicle, all polished and gleaming, with the inscription CAPTURE YOUR DREAMS.

At the sides of the road stood a handful of vendors exposing the vegetables or fruit picked that morning to the exhaust fumes of passing vehicles. Or wooden shacks selling potato chips, water, cookies, pretzels, juices, and chewing gum.

As we drove by, the few people on the street followed us with their eyes. Maybe they thought we were funny or ridiculous. Or maybe they were used to it and looked at us with no more curiosity than you show about a leaf that falls to the ground after being carried along by the wind. At the beginning, for the first few hours, I didn't want to feel like I was part of the group, and I did all I could to think of it as a temporary situation. I thought about the London Olympics in 2012 and I told myself that I had nothing to do with these people. But then I gave in. I accepted the fact that this was my condition now. I had turned into a *journeyer*. I had no choice, if I wanted to survive.

And in any case, we had become a single body.

Each time I shifted, I had to adapt to the five or six people next to me.

Every now and then along the way, we encountered women returning from the fields with huge baskets on their heads, or groups of barefoot children chasing after nothing, who stood dazed as they watched us go by: a jeep jam-packed with people.

Around eleven o'clock that night, after ten hours, we finally stopped. In the middle of nowhere. We had turned onto a side road and followed it for thirty minutes. It was pitch dark. There was nothing anywhere except a shed.

Getting out was much more difficult than getting in.

My joints were stiff; I had a hard time bending my knees and walking. The race. The race flashed in my mind like a bolt from the blue. The older people couldn't straighten their backs. Too many hours with their weight on the sacrum, and some hadn't even been able to rest their feet on the floor of the bed.

With a great deal of effort they made us get out, one by one. A woman who in Addis Ababa had smiled at me encouragingly now looked at me resentfully. She didn't recognize me. Hardened. Everyone seemed much more hardened. Withdrawn inside their armor.

We had to sleep in that shed lit by a single small, central neon fixture. The light was cold and eerie. On the floor, no mattresses. They brought the jeep in as well and closed the door.

Only then did I realize that until that moment I'd been living in suspension, as if I'd been holding my breath since the boy had come to summon me at the apartment in Addis Ababa. When they barred the door from the inside with a big bolt, and I found myself on the floor in a corner without so much as a mat, that's when it hit me.

This was the Journey. Hodan had already gone through it.

In an instant it all came back, along with the urge to vomit.

My body had become accustomed to potholes and abrupt jolts; lying still made my bowels churn. Many people threw up on the floor wherever they happened to be. I recalled people's eyes at the stoplight in Addis Ababa: They'd looked at us as if we were worthless nobodies, as if we were mere things being transported from one place to another.

None of us had said a word; none of us had protested. In the two hours we'd spent locked in that garage in Addis Ababa, with its reek of gasoline and sweat, we had managed to efface our dignity.

Before turning off the light they handed out cereal bars and advised us to get some rest. We would leave again at dawn, in six hours, at five in the morning.

The second day was even worse. The aches and soreness, which until then had been held in check by anger, had all intensified. My right shoulder was giving me excruciating pain. Having to sit still, squashed in without being able to move, was enough to drive you crazy. After a while I began to feel the need to move. I tried and tried; the only thing I was able to do was sit up a little straighter, which was a lifesaver. I was confined in a straitjacket.

Every once in a while someone screamed into the air.

Then, after a while, he quieted down.

We passed only one village, larger than the other two. It must have been market day because the road was lined with a parade of stalls selling clothes, shoes, straw hats, sunglasses, American jeans, motor oil and windshield wipers, women's veils, men's turbans, cucumbers, peaches, lettuce, tomatoes, cookies, milk, Coca-Cola, you name it. It all passed swiftly in front of us like a mirage.

Someone yelled at the driver to stop, but he kept going as if he hadn't heard.

Then the terrain turned to low-lying brush; the trees vanished altogether, giving way to scrub that was all around. Like the ever-present dust that was kicked up as we drove along, coating the jeep and our heads within minutes. That fine powder. I loved it. It was just like the dust that Alì and I used to kick up, which ended up in the old men's *shaat*. I caught myself laughing. The woman next to me looked at me as if I were nuts. She didn't approve of me. She clicked her tongue to say that I was unspeakable. I ignored her. I went on laughing to myself, lulled by memories of being safe.

That night around midnight, one day early, we were told we had arrived.

We were just outside a town and could see some lights in the distance. The men stopped the jeep and ordered us to remain on board. Some people immediately started celebrating, making a racket, thinking we'd made it. They were mistaken.

A man quickly called for silence. We'd better try to understand what the two traffickers were telling us in a language that wasn't ours: a mixture of Arabic and Sudanese. Luckily someone in the group understood Arabic and acted as interpreter.

"We are not in Khartoum," the trafficker said. "We are two kilometers from Al Qadarif, which is just across the border in Sudan. Anyone who doesn't like it can continue on foot."

Without giving us time to react, the two men got back in the jeep and restarted the engine. Al Qadarif is a small town in the desert. The bad news was that we were not where we had paid to go. The good news was that we were no longer in Ethiopia.

They took us to a garage again and, without a word, handed us over to another group of traffickers, who were already there waiting for us. When we went in, we found ourselves facing the same scene as in Addis Ababa. An off-road vehicle and six men who appeared nervous. They smoked and spat on the ground, swearing in a language that none of us understood.

We'd been swindled.

Getting out of the jeep was even more difficult than it had been the day before.

Our bodies were getting used to not responding to commands, to being forced into unnatural, painful positions and to constant, rapid motion.

A couple of men, two Ethiopians, tried to say something. They raised their voices. One was alone; the other was traveling with his wife and three small children. They'd been sitting side by side for hours. Now they were beating their breasts and their heads with their hands, saying things I didn't understand but that didn't seem friendly toward the first traffickers. The latter, ignoring them, restarted the motor and said that anyone who was unhappy was welcome to go back with them.

Immediately. They would even return their money, they said. I couldn't tell if they were kidding or not. In any case, no one budged.

In an instant they were gone, along with the jeep that had been our home for two whole days.

We were left staring at one another, not knowing what to do. I would soon realize that, more than anything else, this is the one thing about the Journey that changes you forever: No one, at any time, can ever know what will happen a moment later.

While we were still standing there, I tried to strike up a conversation with a Somali girl who was traveling with her sister, to have the comfort of a voice. A voice that spoke my language.

Everything had happened so fast. In two days I had forgotten who I was.

"Where are you from?" I asked. "Are you from Mogadishu?" She didn't answer. She kept her eyes on her younger sister, still hunched over on the ground, uncramping her knees and throwing up.

"Are you Somali?" I tried again.

The girl turned around; her face was powdered with white dust up to the hairline, even under the *hijab*. She looked like a ghost, a white mask with lifeless eyes.

"Yes," she replied in a faint voice. Then she bent over her sister and stroked her head.

We soon learned that we needed another two hundred dollars to get to Khartoum.

Another rusty old Land Rover.

We would leave Al Qadarif in a week.

Those who had the money could pay immediately; the others had to find a job or have relatives send the funds to a nearby money-transfer location that they showed us. The traffickers had a satellite phone that could be used to call home. But for those who didn't have the money right then, the two hundred dollars would become two hundred and fifty.

I didn't give it a second's thought; I paid.

For a week I slept in that room on a mattress that was damp from dog or goat piss.

Outside there were hordes of goats, bleating as though possessed at all hours of the day or night: thirsty, starving, crazed like us. May a thousand liters of putrid, stinking water fall on their heads.

CHAPTER 25

※

AFTER A WEEK I set out again. Meanwhile, during those days everything had changed. From that fetid mattress, like a plant that suddenly bears fruit, the seed of self-interest had sprouted. I had begun thinking only of myself. Everything was secondary to my survival. I had become more unsociable, a loner. My only objective was to reach the end of the Journey. I alone had put myself in that situation, and the situation had transformed me. Forever. In just a few days. There was no way I could get out of it, unless I went back on foot. I could only continue. And accept my transformation. I had to make it at all costs. It was no longer about the ultimate goal. It was about survival.

There were fewer of us this time: forty-eight. We were a little less packed; I didn't have the feeling I would pass out each time we hit a pothole.

We all knew that the worst of the Journey was yet to come: crossing the Sahara. Everyone had heard dozens of stories in his lifetime; we knew that the Sahara was the toughest test. For this reason we made every effort not to think about it. In addition, we had rested for a week and we had a little more space. This made us feel foolishly euphoric.

We sang! During that second leg we sang. To pass the time, to mark the hours. The terrain around us didn't help much. There was nothing to see. An endless ocher-colored expanse of nothing. Earth and more earth, everywhere you looked; fine dust that swirled up and got in your throat if you didn't cover your mouth with your veil. Earth and dry brush. And a track, the road we were on, straight as a plumb line, headed north.

We took turns singing the songs of our countries. An Ethiopian woman with her eleven-month-old son in her arms started it off. Her fellow countrymen immediately joined her. Then we Somalis did the same, and finally the Sudanese.

Anything we could, just to avoid thinking. If Hodan had been there, she would have been happy. Who knows, maybe she sang too on her Journey. Maybe she'd been a big hit. Someday she would tell me about it. Not now. It makes no sense to think further than what you see in front of you. The future doesn't exist.

After driving for twenty hours we stopped again, in front of a brick building surrounded only by dusty desert. All around us, nothing. It was night, but it had been at least six hours since we'd seen anything but earth and rocks. Rocks and earth. Then, abruptly, the low brush merged with the soil, and soon everything turned to sand. Actual fine sand. Without realizing it we had crossed into the Sahara.

It was the singing. That's what it had done for us.

We soon learned that once again we were not in Khartoum but in a village that we were told was called Sharif al Amin. This driver and his backup also spoke only Sudanese and a little Arabic. Again several among us acted as interpreters.

They told us that the jeep had broken down and that we'd been forced to stop.

You catch on quickly enough on the Journey.

The truth is irrelevant to those who have fled and are in need of refuge. That jeep hadn't broken down; that jeep was running just fine. But we wanted to believe it, simply because we wanted to get out and stretch our legs, straighten our backs. The truth is traded for survival. For a trifle. For naught.

Only one Somali man got angry. He was thin and looked like an intellectual: He wore wire-rimmed glasses, the lenses coated with a layer of dust, which he must have been used to.

"You're all a bunch of filthy crooks," he said in Arabic. "Thieves and bastards! Two-bit swindlers," he ranted, foaming at the mouth.

The backup driver went over to him and gave him a loud smack. The man fell to the ground. His glasses broke, cracked in half. Struggling to get up with the two broken pieces in his hand, he kept it up: "You're disgusting. Filthy two-bit scammers." The trafficker kicked him in the calf and made him fall again. "Shut up, *hawaian*," he told him. Animal.

And that was that.

We were in their hands.

They knew it; they'd learned how to tell when a man turns into a *needy refugee*. They read it in your eyes. It's something that shows. Plain as the rising sun, clear as flowing water. It's something you carry with you, written in your eyes. You can try all you want to hide it, but you'll never be able to. It's the smell of a downtrodden animal.

There, for the first time, we were called animals. When you enter the desert, you stop being a human being. I had been a *tahrib* in Addis Ababa, but now I was a needy *tahrib* refugee. A vulnerable illegal. An animal tethered to life by an ever-more-tenuous thread.

They beat you.

If you don't have the money, they beat you.

If you don't obey orders, they beat you.

If you dare to respond, they beat you.

If you ask for more water, they beat you. They don't care if you're a man or a woman, an adult or a child: They beat you.

If you protest, they bring you to the police.

And there you have only two options. Pay the police to be handed over to other traffickers, or let them take you back to the border with Ethiopia.

Early in the Journey you learn to keep silent and pray.

Early in the Journey you learn to forget why you're there and to practice silence and prayer.

For ten days I stayed in Sharif al Amin, in that brick house that was actually a prison with bars on the windows. Two liters of water every twenty-four hours, and two servings of food. A mattress on the floor in quarters for thirty people.

To get to Khartoum, another two hundred dollars were needed.

I had almost run out of money.

On the third day I called Hodan in Finland and revealed that I had left. She thought I was still in Addis Ababa; I hadn't wanted to tell anyone. I had only one minute's time, not a second more. She knew. That's what the traffickers allow you on their satellite phones. A minute doesn't seem like very much, but in that situation it becomes timeless. In a minute you can say everything you need. You learn that a minute can save your life. That's all you need.

Hodan wasn't expecting me; speaking in rapid-fire bursts she told me to be careful, to try to become friendly with the Somalis, to always stay in a group, never to go off on my own, to do as the others did so I wouldn't stand out. Suddenly my brain started functioning again; I took in everything she said.

She asked me where I was and I told her.

She hadn't been there; she didn't know the place. Her Journey had taken a different route.

I told her I needed money to continue, that I had used up what I had, and that I didn't want to call Hooyo or Said; I didn't want them to worry. I would call them from Italy once I got there.

I told her where to send the money.

Before ending the call she reminded me not to be afraid.

"Never say you're afraid, Samia."

"Okay, *abaayo*."

Never.

It was what I used to tell her during her Journey.

But everything was different now. I *was* afraid; I was very afraid. Frayed. I felt frayed. Like the worn photo of Mo Farah stuffed in my bag; I felt as fragile as butterfly wings. As insubstantial as a cloud. *Poof.*

What a lot of things you can say in a minute. A lot.

The money from Hodan arrived after eight days, and two nights later I resumed the Journey.

CHAPTER 26

WHEN I GOT TO KHARTOUM, I knew I had to rest up and recoup my strength for the hardest part, crossing the Sahara.

I was shattered. I was a memory of myself, not a presence, a slender thread of memories and scattered images. That's all I was.

I stayed in a tiny apartment on the outskirts south of the city for six weeks, along with thirty other women. A month and a half. All we did was sleep and take turns going out to buy food at the market or in a store a short distance from the house. We were *tahrib;* we had to be careful. We crept around like *tahrib*. We were shifty-eyed like *tahrib*. We looked like paranoid, frantic mice, always on guard. In danger of being sent back to where we'd started.

I had to call Hodan again and have her send me another five hundred dollars for a leg of the trip that was supposed to get me to Tripoli. Reluctantly, I was having her give me back Alì's money that I had sent her for Mannaar. But things had changed. Mannaar came to me in my dreams and no longer in my waking thoughts. Awake, all I thought of was staying alive.

And no one had told me that the Journey would be so expensive.

I knew they wouldn't take us to Tripoli, that they would leave us someplace else. But I had learned. If I didn't want fear to get the better of me, what I had to do was not think about it.

I spent forty days stuck in that apartment in a six-story building on the ugly outskirts of Khartoum. There were only two windows, and all you could see was the concrete facades of other dilapidated buildings like ours. Flaking walls and decrepit balconies. In the distance, as far as you could see, a patch of desert could be glimpsed between two buildings.

Golden.

The heat was asphyxiating. And there were thirty-one women and three children in very cramped quarters. I spent the first ten days lying on the ground on a mat.

I didn't even have enough air to dream.

Then I made a mistake.

In spite of everything, maybe I still felt like I was invulnerable, invincible, the Samia I'd always been. True, I had effaced myself and struggled to even remember who I was; memories flashed by only when they chose to. But maybe what we are deep inside can't be effaced. Maybe that's how it is, and we end up recognizing who we are only through what we do. Anyway, Ayana, a Somali girl, warned me not to do it. But the water was all used up, and we were waiting for the sun to go down to go out and buy some containers. I was parched. That night I'd sweated so profusely that the moisture had drenched my clothes and soaked through to the hard mat. I drank tap water from the bathroom. Within three hours I began to feel strong shudders running down my back, along my arms and legs, everywhere. Cold sweats. Then nausea and hallucinations. I was gripped by a fever I'd never experienced before. And dysentery. Since I'd left, I hadn't eaten much. The muscles I had developed with Eshetu were slowly wasting away. I could see for myself. The dysentery was the final blow.

I spent twenty days on the mat in a comatose state. Ayana comforted me. She remained healthy while others fell ill as I did. If it wasn't the water, it could be an unwashed fruit. Or a fruit rinsed with that same water. Or some rotten fish.

I should have left sooner, but I waited to get my strength back. Ayana had no one to call in Europe for money, so she would remain in that house much longer than I. She'd almost begun to think of it as home.

Then, finally, I was well again. I'd recovered my strength. At least as much as I needed.

They squeezed us all in, only this time there were even more of us than the first time. Eighty-six. So packed in that we gagged for lack of air. Once again a jeep.

After a few kilometers no one spoke anymore, no one complained, no one even thought of singing. The stretch through the desert is much tougher. The heat is so intense you could die, and besides that, the vehicle proceeds more slowly, maintaining a constant low speed. It doesn't brake or accelerate, so as not to get stuck in the sand. Everything is grueling, even breathing. It's like crawling along on an endless road at a snail's pace. As you move ahead, you can see the road lengthen rather than shorten.

That leg was supposed to last four days. We waited only for the times when the jeep would stop, twice a day. Once, in daylight, to do our business and sip some water. The other, at night, to sleep on the sand. The days had turned into a single, endless, prolonged waiting. From the moment you set out again, you started counting the minutes until the next stop.

All around, a lunar landscape in which earth and sky are one. Your points of reference vanish. It's like diving into a mirror. An endless expanse of sand. So uniform that you too end up turning into sand. And not just because it filters in everywhere, so that it quickly fills your eyes, throat, and lungs with grit, and you have to swallow so it won't clog up your mouth. Soon you stop fighting it and simply close your eyes, clamp your jaws shut, and count. You count to a thousand, and at every hundred you swallow what little saliva you have left, keeping count with your fingers. You know that when you get to a thousand, twenty minutes will have passed. Amir, a Somali, taught this to me on the first leg of the trip from Addis Ababa to Al Qadarif. Then you count to ten thousand. That comes to over three hours. When you've counted to ten thousand three times, it's almost time for the stop. Going on like that, you too end up becoming sand, because you see yourself as a minute grain of that white expanse, or as one of the seconds of time that, like a madwoman, you can't get out of your head.

I kept my plastic bag tucked under my T-shirt.

We had ten liters of water per person for four days. Two and a half liters a day, which in the intense heat of the Sahara aren't enough for even a few hours.

Every so often someone would fall asleep or pass out from lack of air. It happened to me too. The woman next to me, an old Somali, noticed it and tried to wake me up by nudging me with her shoulders, but I didn't respond. Then someone who had managed to hide a bottle of water pulled it out. They passed the word and in a few minutes the bottle reached the woman. She poured a little on my head and I came to. What had happened to my strength? Where was the little Olympic warrior? Had I really been in Beijing, or was it all a dream? The opening ceremony, with me a bright star in the firmament of the strongest in the whole world? And Mo Farah in the middle of the field, laughing and relaxed? Another hallucination?

In the evening we traveled until even the drivers were ready to drop. To avoid being seen by police helicopters patrolling the desert, the traffickers keep the lights turned off, using them as little as possible. You're in the Sahara at night with no light, crushed among dozens of bodies on a dilapidated jeep creeping along like a snail.

As soon as the sun went down it felt like we were traveling in a nightmare. Counting relaxed me and fed my imagination. Every now and then I thought I was on a plane, like when I went to Beijing and took the sleeping pill. As it had then, the constant noise of the engine made me dream of being in an endless, dark tunnel. Suddenly I opened my eyes and everything slipped away. I was going to China; they were my Olympics. The hotel would be beautiful. I would shake hands with Veronica Campbell-Brown. She would look at me curiously at first, then with admiration. I would run in a huge stadium in front of TV cameras from around the world. I would give it my best. At the end everyone would stand up to applaud me, journalists from throughout the world would interview me, my face would be seen in every corner of the planet.

Then a sharp bump, an abrupt swerve, or a deep depression, someone vomiting. I was plunged back to where I was. In a dark tunnel that wasn't a dream. Hours and hours without headlights, guided only by GPS.

Eighty-six of us clinging to the technology of a GPS.

There are no roads in the Sahara. There are no tracks. Each trafficker on each Journey follows his own particular route. In the morning the tire marks are covered over by sand. Erased forever. No Journey is the same as another.

For days you're in the hands of human traffickers who in turn are in the hands of a small box that communicates with a satellite.

Around three in the morning we'd stop someplace in the midst of that expanse of sand dunes, eat *moffa*, a grain and corn-flour mush, and try to get some sleep; we lay there huddled around that rusted vehicle, which from outside seemed minuscule.

The families stayed together, the children crying. The older people moaned and groaned.

I had become friends with an Ethiopian girl, Zena, a little older than me, who wanted to be a doctor. Her dream was to get to Europe and enroll in college. Any university in any European city—to her it made no difference. She was traveling with her elderly grandmother, who was always glued to her.

In spite of everything, we couldn't sleep. It was difficult to sleep. Many people prayed. They prayed out loud. The children were never still and the parents didn't know what to do. There was one child in particular, Said, four years old, with his mother and father. Said seemed possessed. He cried all day and didn't stop, not even at night. He never stopped. Given the way he kept crying, making his throat sore and scratchy, his voice had become hoarse and croaky, like that of a muttering, demented old man or an abandoned dog tied to a post for weeks. The parents did their best to keep him quiet. Every night they had to take turns moving a distance away in order not to disturb the group. Otherwise someone might go berserk. You had to be careful about everything.

On those nights, lying on the sand with the aimless, dark forms of the desert cockroaches and beetles, I thought about Hooyo and I thought about Aabe. I cried and silently begged my father for help. Or I talked to Hodan, telling her that I would be with her soon. I thought about Beijing, the happy days, about that first morning at the hotel in front of the BBC. About the applause, the fans standing and shouting my name.

I focused on the upcoming London Olympics and tried to bear up.

By doing that, I was slowly able to fall asleep.

At noon, after driving for two days, the Land Rover broke down, this time for real.

It started jolting and jerking for a while; then it got mired in the sand. We were in the middle of the Sahara with brutal heat and no protection.

We all got out. The traffickers tried to disassemble a few parts without letting anyone get near the engine. After three hours they realized that there was nothing they could do and called for help, transmitting the coordinates of the GPS.

The children were already crying; the elderly tried to take cover in the meager shade under the jeep. We were stranded there for twenty-four hours. The water had been used up long ago. We thought we would all die, and that individual thought became a collective one. Somehow, all of a sudden, everyone began to buckle under the same pressure, as if a huge mallet had materialized and begun pounding down on all our heads simultaneously.

The endless hours stretched out in hallucinations: Sitting on the sand without protection, those visions became a common delirium.

Then the sound of an engine was heard in the distance. We didn't know if it was real or imaginary. But before long the silhouette of a vehicle appeared from behind a dune. They had found us. And they also had water; there were lots of jerricans tied to the outside.

That same evening we resumed the trek.

You quickly become ruthless. Everyone thinks only of himself.

No one tells you this before; you learn for yourself that it's up to you not to fall out of the jeep. If you fall off, the traffickers won't stop. They tell you that right away, before the start of each stretch.

There are only three rules, the same for every trip, and each time they're repeated.

Number one: You can't take anything with you but the plastic bag.

Number two: If at any time you rebel against the conditions of the Journey and force the vehicle to stop, you will be left where you are.

Number three: If you fall out of the jeep, the driver will not stop.

This last rule is meant to prevent hang-ups. It's not like they would lose too much time. All they'd have to do is stop, pick up the person who fell off, shove him back into the jeep bed, and be on their way again. Yet that's not what happens. If you fall, you won't be rescued. If you knew that you could let go, many people would do it. Within a few hours the others would get discouraged.

After a few days in the intense heat, the insignificant ants that we are would rise up. Better to stir everyone up against one another and avoid the risk of having the tires get stuck in the sand.

And besides, you're just a *hawaian,* an animal, who pays to be transported from one place to another, nothing more. In fact, for the traffickers you're evidence of the crime if they should be stopped by the police. Every complication means a loss of time.

On the last morning Zena and her grandmother ended up at the back of the jeep bed. We had slept a distance away from the vehicle to steer clear of little Said, who wouldn't stop crying. When they called us at dawn, we knew we had to get a move on; otherwise we would be left for last. The grandmother could hardly walk: She'd sprained her ankle; maybe her foot had been in the wrong position for too many long hours. I ran ahead to save a place for them. But someone started yelling, saying I couldn't hold places for anyone else, everyone had to fend for himself. I said something about an elderly lady, and an Ethiopian woman started shrieking, threatening to slap me if I didn't stop it. She sat down next to me. I tried to move back but there was no way; the mass of humanity was too dense. I had to stay where I was. I called out loudly to Zena, and from the back she told me not to worry: They had found seats.

All of a sudden, after a few hours, someone shouted something in a language that wasn't mine. Perhaps Arabic, perhaps Ethiopian, maybe Sudanese or English. Then someone up front started pounding his fist on the roof of the driver's cab.

"Stop! Stop!"

I thought someone felt sick; it happened occasionally. The

driver went straight on as if he hadn't heard. The man kept on banging and banging. After a while the trafficker lowered the window and stuck out his arm, his open hand facing the jeep bed in the Arabic gesture that means "Go to hell." Shove it!

Then word passed from ear to ear.

Someone had fallen out. Zena's grandmother had fallen out.

CHAPTER 27

THEY DROPPED US OFF AT the Libyan border. It was October 12, 2011.

The Land Rover stopped and we waited there.

I don't know how they knew that Sudan ended at that particular spot, since we were surrounded by nothing but sand. In any case, Sudan ended there. We waited for hours.

Then they came to pick us up.

Libyan traffickers.

Much worse than the Sudanese, so everyone said. Because in Libya the law is more severe.

They showed up, loaded us onto a small bus, and took us to the prison in Kufra.

Our worst nightmare had materialized.

We all knew what Kufra was. A place where you were likely to stay forever, if you didn't have the money they demanded— and it was a lot of money. Or else when you started stinking like a corpse, they took you back to the border with Sudan, just before you died. They left you in the middle of the Sahara to drop dead there.

That's what everyone said.

Our arrival, however, was not traumatic. The place was better than the prison in Sharif al Amin: bigger, more spacious. A light-colored building of rough concrete blocks, it stood right in the middle of the desert.

All around, the usual endless expanse of golden sand dunes. We breathed the smell of dust, stirred by a slight breeze that drifted in through the gate, which the guards left open during the day. When we first arrived, we were treated well. They separated the women from the men and they brought us as much food and water as we wanted. They washed me. Dressed me in new clothes. They said, "Welcome to Libya." They put me on a mattress, and after weeks with my back on the sand it was a blessing.

All this, however, lasted two days.

At the end of the second day they came back and demanded money.

A thousand dollars to take me to Tripoli.

As usual, if I didn't have it I could make a call. One minute maximum.

They came five times a day to remind me to pay. Five times with sticks and their "*Hafta, hawaian*," "Pay, animal." Until I paid. It can go on for weeks, months. They don't care; they don't give up. But only if you're clever enough to make them believe that sooner or later you will pay.

When they realize that you're one of those who won't pay, there are only two possibilities.

If you're a man, they'll take you back to the border.

If you're a woman, they'll rape you in exchange for a one-way ticket. This is what I was told by Taliya, a Somali girl, the third day after I arrived. I could tell she was from my country, and I needed to talk to someone, to feel the consolation of a voice, to talk freely with another human being. We slept next to each other, and that day I ran into her in the communal yard and spoke to her. "What's your name? Are you Somali?" I asked, sitting down next to her on a bench against the clay wall. She kept her eyes lowered. Who knows at what point in the Journey she'd lost the nerve to look people in the eye?

I repeated the question: "What's your name?"

She wouldn't speak. But I persisted.

After a while she said, "Taliya," then continued staring at the ground. I started asking her the dumbest questions; I just felt like talking. Taliya didn't answer anymore. I kept it up like a raving lunatic for half an hour, maybe an hour. I wanted her to answer. Finally all she said was: "I let them fuck me like a dog to get out of here. I've been in this place for four months."

It took Hodan twenty-eight days to wire the money to me at a small wooden shack for the transfer of cash that coincidentally stood at the entrance to the prison. Twenty-eight endless days in which I lived on water and peanuts. After the first forty-eight hours, in fact, they didn't give us anything else, just water and peanuts. Like monkeys. If you had money you could buy something directly from the guards. But if you had money they came and took it from you as an advance on the thousand dollars.

The prison was divided into two sections, male and female. There was a shared yard where we could walk around and breathe in the dusty desert wind. Nothing ever happened. We were depleted, reduced to shadows of ourselves. No one spoke; some ranted and raved due to the heat or the solitude, longing for home. I tried to keep calm and stay out of trouble.

One day four Ethiopian men who'd been in Kufra for five months decided to get together and teach the guards a lesson, after having been beaten by them numerous times. They knew they'd end up getting the worst of it, but by now they were out of their heads; they wanted to lash out, get a taste of hammering someone. Word of what was about to happen had spread; this was the only kind of thing we told one another about. It was our entertainment; our lives played out on the edge of survival. At two in the afternoon we gathered in the yard to witness the settling of scores. Two guards were the cruelest: When they beat you, they did it to inflict pain, to leave marks. Two of the Ethiopians called them over with some excuse. Grumbling, the guards sauntered over in their short-sleeved green uniforms, clubs and guns in their belts. The other two Ethiopians immediately came up and surrounded them, kicking and punching wildly, until the guards fell to the ground. The Ethiopians let it all out, unleashing on the two guards all the hatred they'd nurtured for months. Before long, however, six other guards ran up. One of the two on the ground was barely moving, completely covered in blood, while the other one appeared to be dead, lying motionless, his eyes wide open. I watched, anesthetized, inured to it by now. The blazing sun had shriveled my brain. Nothing shocked me. One of the six bent down and felt his fellow officer's pulse. He must have been dead. They asked who'd killed him. No one breathed a word. They asked again. Nothing. The one in command, the smallest of all, pulled out his gun and fired into the air. He asked again. One of the Ethiopians, the heaviest one, stepped forward. "I was the one who killed," he said in Arabic. The little man in uniform ordered him to kneel down, right there in front of everyone. Then he asked him to confirm it. "I was the one who killed," the Ethiopian repeated. We all knew what was coming. No one closed his eyes or looked away. The Ethiopian knew it too; he didn't turn a hair. The commander leveled his gun. A single shot, point-blank. The Ethiopian joined the other man on the ground.

I spent twenty-eight endless days prowling around like a ghost among ghosts. At night I couldn't sleep because of the heat, and during the day I tortured myself, weak as I was, looking for a corner with a speck of shade. I wanted to train, do some exercises, stretch my muscles leaning against the wall. But the peanuts weren't enough; I had no energy. My vision clouded over; when the sun was at its peak, I had hallucinations. Sitting on the ground, my back against a wall, I saw Aabe, the courtyard, the eucalyptus. I thought I was up there with Alì, hidden among the cool branches. Or on the mattress in the evening, holding Hodan's hand tightly. I didn't even have the money to call her or Hooyo.

There was nothing I could do except sit there and wait. With the part of my brain that remained alert, I felt that I was slowly but surely losing touch with myself. I was giving up; I no longer had the strength. At times I thought it didn't matter to me: I would stay there on the ground forever.

Then too, day and night, I would dream about delicious foods. The breakfast buffet at the hotel in Beijing. It had everything: fruit juices, hard-boiled or scrambled eggs, sausages, beans, mushrooms, tomatoes, coffee, tea, cappuccino, hot chocolate, croissants, biscuits with honey, toast, cold cuts, cheeses. And someone to serve me. Every day I went over that food in my mind. And to think I hadn't even tried it all. I sat there for days, out of my mind. I was out of my mind.

Until the money from Hodan arrived and I paid.

Finally I could go, I could leave Kufra.

Then they showed me what would be my home for the next week of the Journey.

A freight container with no light and just a small opening at the top to let air in. I would share it with two hundred and twenty other people. Without saying a word, now as worn-out as the tattered rags we wore, we climbed in.

Being in a container is like being in a gas chamber. The sun heats the metal walls to such a degree that after a few hours everything is vaporized. Breath, urine, feces, vomit, sweat. Everything evaporates in a toxic cloud that obstructs your breathing.

For the first stretch, maybe half an hour, we stood, as if we were about to get off at any moment: We didn't know how to act, what to do. Then we sat on the floor, and we soon learned that the only way to support your back was to lean against someone else's body.

The metal sheets of the walls were scorching hot, like fire. We tried to stay as close to the center as possible to keep away from the heat that was inescapable; it stole your breath and erased your thoughts. When we were little and got sick, Hooyo would put mint leaves and rosemary in a pot of water and boil it. Then she would make us lean over it for hours, our heads covered with a cloth, so we could inhale the steam and clear our noses and our heads. At the end we would be dripping, all our pores open. Being in the container was a thousand times worse; it was like being in the boiling pot itself. The floor too was flaming hot. We tried to keep our knees bent, so that only our shoes (for those who still had them) touched the metal. But you can't stay in the same position for hours, so we took turns straightening our legs. The relief was so great that we put up with burning our thighs. The flesh bright red like blood.

The only way to survive was to climb over the others in turn and stick your nose out of the opening for a few seconds. After two hours without oxygen, before blacking out, you have hallucinations. Visual, auditory. We needy *tahrib* refugees, penned in that container, talked to people who existed in our eyes only, screamed at people who shouted in our ears only.

Being caged in the container opens your eyes to people's foolishness. After a few hours there are no more gender differences. Men and women are all the same; you are reduced to the lowest common denominator. All that remains of you is a shadow struggling to survive. You no longer even remember whether you're a woman or a man. There may have been a few Ethiopian Christians in the container, but the majority of people were Muslim. Yet none of the women had her legs or head covered. Everything showing, everything exposed, because there's nothing left anymore except that body that only a detail or two reminds you is yours. The mole you have on your thigh. The crooked toes on your feet. The scar on your belly. You're you. But you're also no longer you, dissolved into the vapors of other bodies. When the stranger next to you can't hold his bowels, or when you can't, and you go on breathing and journeying for days in that nauseating stench, with no food or water, you no longer even know who you were before. The image of my mother on Hodan's wedding day as she takes my face in her hands, her eyes swollen with tears, and tells me: "You look beautiful, my daughter. You're the most beautiful one in the family." My awkwardness at being all dressed up in those colored veils, the white *hijab* wrapped around my head and shoulders. The first time I saw myself as feminine, the first time I felt special.

Maybe I was nobody anymore. Maybe I had always been made of the stuff of dreams.

On the third day in the container, a forty-two-year-old man, a Somali, died. The woman next to him noticed it, after who knows how long. For two days they'd been trying to give him water from a bottle that had appeared out of nowhere, but he could no longer swallow.

He'd stayed in Kufra only one afternoon; he had the money for the leg to Tripoli with him. Most likely he was feeling sick and had decided to get to the city as soon as possible. His throat had become clogged as a result of the sand he'd inhaled on the jeep in the desert. The granules had formed a dense plug that the water couldn't get through.

He died of suffocation. When the news spread through the container, whispered from ear to ear as usual, without anyone's saying a word we intoned the Salat Al-Janaza, the prayer for the dead. Each in his own language. We accompanied that man, whose name I never even knew, on his personal journey.

That night when we stopped to sleep, we dug a hole in the sand and we buried the body in the earth that had longed to take him back.

Every so often, as I sat like a limp sack on the metal floor that burned like fire, leaning against someone, the London Olympics came to mind. That's what kept me alive: the urge to set my legs in motion, to let my muscles explode. It was the only way I managed to survive. I dreamed about the coach I would have once I got to Europe. For some reason I imagined him to be the coach Mo Farah had. I saw myself in England before reaching Helsinki. I measured my times, seeing them improve week after week, day after day.

I saw myself in the final.

I pictured the fans standing up and applauding. This time because I had finished first.

But instead . . . Instead of Tripoli they took us to another prison, just outside the town of Ajdabiya.

Yet another scam.

To leave there I would need fifteen hundred dollars, which was a lot even for Hodan and Omar. I stayed there for almost two months.

I *had* to reach my destination. And in the end I gave in. I called Hooyo to ask for money from her and from my siblings too, confessing that I'd left on the Journey but lying and saying that everything was fine. I told her that we had only one minute, not to cry, everything was going well, I was happy and I even found time to train. In a short time I would reach Hodan. By then I no longer even believed it myself. It had been five months since I'd left Addis Ababa, and it all seemed hopeless.

In the prison of Ajdabiya they treated us better than in Kufra, but two prison police robbed me of seven hundred and fifty dollars. Actually, you pay the police, not the traffickers. These are the same police who sell you to those who will take you to the next destination. In my case they'd demanded fifteen hundred dollars when they'd asked others for seven hundred and fifty instead. They had dug in their heels, adamant. If I hadn't agreed, they would have done to me what they'd done to other girls who were alone: They would have raped me. Like Taliya.

All I could do was wait.

Pray, wait, and read. In fact there were letters in that prison. In Arabic, in Somali, in Ethiopian, and in English, left there somehow, for some reason, tossed aside in a corner, accumulated over years and years. Letters from prisoners or from their loved ones. Maybe they were mementos of the dead that the guards had never had the nerve to discard. In those letters there were lives. And so, reading them, I rediscovered what no longer existed inside of me. Life. Memories. Love. Promises. Courage. Hope. There were some from a man who wrote to his wife every day. Each morning when the sun rose. A young woman who, dreaming, wrote hopeful words to her two-year-old son, who'd been left in Somalia. A little boy who asked his father and mother to be brave, in letters that were never delivered. They were orphaned words, which had never reached their destination. I liked to think that they were meant for me.

In those two months all I did was read and sleep. I hadn't had the energy to train for some time. If the individuals who had written those yellowed letters had had the strength to write what they'd written, I could make it too. I reread them continually, learning my favorite passages by heart.

There was also an Internet connection. I had a young Somali man lend me a few cents, and every now and then I e-mailed Hodan. In the days that followed, I lived in expectation of her reply. She told me that everything was fine in Helsinki and that she couldn't wait for me to get there. She cheered me up, telling me to remember that it would all be over soon.

Lying on the hard, tick-infested mat, I asked myself if it was all worth it. My answer was no. Why had I let myself in for this? All I wanted was to be a two-hundred-meter champion. No one in the world, over the brief course of his life, should have to go through this hell.

One evening a group of three Somali men escaped from the prison. The guards had forgotten to bolt the door. I'd met one of the three men, Abdullahi, a couple of weeks ago; he'd lent me the money for the Internet. I'd told him my story. He remembered the race in Beijing. He said his wife had told him about me. She had remained in Mogadishu; he would support her, sending her money every month, once he got to Italy. We'd become friends. We talked, we confided in each other, and occasionally we ate together. At first he didn't believe it was me; he thought I'd made it all up. It didn't seem possible that I had been reduced to sleeping with fleas in a prison in the Libyan desert.

The guards brought us supper, rice and vegetables and half a liter of water; then they left for the night. That evening they hadn't locked up, and Abdullahi came to me and asked if I wanted to join them. They would escape when night fell and walk to the town of Ajdabiya. The following morning they would find a way to get to Tripoli from there. It wasn't complicated, but if they were caught, they'd be killed.

I had to decide. I had only two hours and I couldn't talk about it to anyone.

Five months ago I would have said yes. That evening I said no to Abdullahi. I think Aabe was pleased with me. I would stay there and wait for money from Hodan and Hooyo.

The men left two hours later and we never heard anything more about them.

Then, at last, the money came. I left the letters to a sweet Somali girl who had just arrived, depleted and tearful. I told her that reading them would save her life. There they were and no one paid any attention to them. Yet it was only thanks to them that I had survived that prison.

I was alive, in fact, and free at last. I would travel with nine other people in the trailer of a truck carrying sacks of corn flour. The most comfortable leg of the Journey.

Still sleeping in the trailer, we made a two-day stop in Sirte to wait for a few other *tahrib*.

Then we set off again.

Finally, after a week, I was in Tripoli.

It was December 15, 2011. Exactly five months since my departure from Addis Ababa. A year after leaving Mogadishu.

I was free.

When we heard the sounds of the city from inside the trailer, we began to cry. Ten wraiths weeping silently inside the trailer of a truck. Ten wraiths who were ashamed of their tears. All the same, those tears brought us together. That's what happens when you cry as one. I will always carry with me those nine tearful faces. They will always be my brothers and I their sister. I realized that I hadn't cried in months. The desert had drained me of everything, even my tears, my saliva. It had drunk them all up.

When we stopped in a big square and they told us to get out,

I felt light as air. I could barely stand on my feet, but by some miracle my brain began to function.

They abandoned us in that busy square; it was almost sunset, and several stalls selling sweets and kebabs were closing up. Ten wraiths covered with sand, smelly and filthy like pigs.

Ten wraiths among the Libyan inhabitants.

The traffickers opened the trailer and said: "You're free."

Then they climbed back into the cab and drove off, raising a big cloud of dust and leaving us there to breathe the diesel fumes that by now were part of our lungs.

We found ourselves lost. And famished.

No, we found ourselves.

I was free.

Free as the air, free as waves breaking in the sea.

CHAPTER 28

✿

IN TRIPOLI I LIVED for almost a month in the Somali district. All of us Somali and Ethiopian *tahrib* waiting to embark for Italy occupied about a dozen buildings crowded together in the same neighborhood east of the city. An ugly, dirty area fit for illegals and sewer rats like us. Yet from the very first moment my arrival in Tripoli was a liberation. I never wanted to see the desert again for the rest of my life; that much I was sure of.

There was nothing I hated more than the desert. When you spend months there, the desert gets into your bones, your blood, your saliva; you can't ever get it out of you. You carry the dust everywhere; even if you wash with running water it stays with you forever. But the worst thing is that the desert extinguishes your soul, it obliterates your thoughts. You have to close your eyes and imagine things that aren't there. Months and months of stretches of sand. Wherever you turn, at whatever time of day or night. Only sand and nothing but sand. It drives you insane.

Once I got to Tripoli, I realized that it was a miracle that I'd survived. It was only thanks to those yellowed letters and to the Olympics that I'd come through sane and not stark, raving mad. It's only when you see the light after being in the dark a long time that you remember the color of things.

That's what happened to me. I remembered what the world was like. And I loved it.

We lived in cramped rooms. Thirty or forty people in each apartment. I was with forty women from all over Africa: All the illegal emigrants meet up in Tripoli. There were Nigerians, Congolese, Somalis, Ethiopians, Sudanese, women from Namibia, Ghana, Togo, the Ivory Coast, Biafra, Liberia. Adults, adolescents, young women, little girls, old ladies. All together and finally safe.

We felt safe. We were in a city; there was everything we needed to live: water, fruit, food. It was all there and no one would snatch it away from us or beat us. I would have stayed in Tripoli for a lifetime, as many thought they'd do once they got there, if it hadn't been for the fact that we were *tahrib* and the police had it in for us as a result of agreements made between the Libyan and Italian governments. If caught, we were to be sent back to our own countries. We knew that.

Nevertheless, we weren't interested in living undercover in those days. If we'd made it that far—some in two months, some in two years, some, like me, in five months—if we had overcome the Sahara, if we were survivors, all we could think of at that point was reaching our destination. Only the destination. Everything else was eclipsed. For us *tahrib* in Tripoli there was only that one goal. Tripoli for us was a transit point, a faint breath of wind, the rustling of a leaf, the blink of an eye.

Then too, in Tripoli there's the sea. The city, like Mogadishu, is awash with the scent of the sea. That's why my energy returned, the desire to live and take pleasure in life. But there too, as in Mogadishu, I could not go to the sea; if they caught me I would be arrested. I would have to wait; I would just have to wait to get to Italy.

And so, along with food, the urge for companionship came back, to eat together, tell one another our stories, take turns planning our future. And talking. Words are lifesavers. And the words uttered by far the most, by each in his own distorted accent, were "Italy" and "Lampedusa."

Never in my life have I loved talking as much as I did during the long period I spent in Tripoli. We formed teams according to nationality and challenged one another at cards: Each taught the others their own ways of playing, and then we argued over the rules. We taught one another words in our respective languages. We talked about our families, our homes, our parents, our brothers and sisters, our sweethearts. Our favorite dishes. We wondered how awful the food would be in Europe. We wondered what the people would be like. We imagined the houses we would have. The kitchens. The bathrooms with a tub and shower. Carpeting on the floor, or parquet. And what we would do, our work. I would be an athlete. There were some who dreamed of being lawyers, some teachers, others nurses or pediatricians. Some just wanted a family. We passed the time together, talking about our respective plans. And we also thought about practical things. Like how we would leave. For the last time.

The routine for crossing the sea was the usual. You arrange for the money for the voyage; then you wait. You wait for them to come and call you and tell you, with no time to prepare, you're leaving in an hour.

You know that anything can happen at sea, but you don't think about it. All you think about is the destination. If all goes well, in two days, two and a half at most, you'll be in Lampedusa. But anything can happen. The sea is a bigger obstacle than the Sahara; the traffickers tell you that when you contact them.

I went with two other Somali girls.

"Prepare for the worst," they tell you. "What you've faced so far is nothing. By comparison, the Sahara is a cakewalk," they tell you. And you don't believe it. It can't be true. What I had faced up to that point was hell, nothing could be worse. Besides, the sea, *my* sea, couldn't hurt me. We'd had a rendezvous planned for nearly twenty years now. I knew it and the sea knew it. In Italy, at last, we would meet up. One of the first things I'd do was plunge into it and enjoy that vast, welcoming immensity.

The boats are old pieces of junk that should be used only for scrap iron. The sea's power is capable of engulfing them at any moment. For us *tahrib*, however, they were pure gold, luxurious cruise yachts. In addition to engine failures, the trafficker might get lost; the damn GPS could fail or make a mistake. Or we might even run out of gas; it seems impossible but it happens: Sometimes they miscalculate the amount of fuel they need, or they unintentionally extend the route and are left empty. You know that anything can happen but you don't think about it; what you think about is the destination.

There you are, waiting for that moment for weeks or months, and when it comes you're caught unprepared. Every time. There's no way to prepare; I don't know anyone who was ever prepared. Not in terms of what you need to bring with you: There are only two or three things and they are always with you. No, prepared in your head. Prepared for the fact that it's the end of the Journey.

You don't know if it will be morning, afternoon, or night. It's usually at night, but you can never tell; it depends on the trafficker's strategy. There are some who decide on midnight, so they can be offshore before the light. Some opt for the afternoon, so they can already be far out to sea by daybreak. Others instead choose the early morning, so they can cover a long distance and be far away from Africa when darkness falls, and therefore less visible.

I was hoping my voyage would be in the afternoon; it seemed like a quieter time to start out.

I was jittery; Hodan had told me that she would promptly send the money I needed, twelve hundred dollars, to the address I had given her. I couldn't wait.

It didn't even take a month. I don't know how Hodan came up with the money, but I didn't care; it was one of the things I'd ask her once I got there.

My turn came a few days later, on January 12, 2012. It wasn't in the afternoon. It was in the morning, at 4:00 a.m. I was awakened and told to leave.

But my trip lasted only three hours. That's how short-lived my joy at being at sea was. We hardly had time to board—seventy of us in a rubber dinghy that was too small—when we had to turn back. The air that morning was electric; the sun wouldn't rise until two hours later and the excitement among us was so tense you could cut it with a knife. We settled into our places in silence, some on the outside, some in the middle. I ended up at the stern on the outside next to the traffickers; because I was skinny I squeezed in between two hefty Nigerian guys whose arms were as big as my legs.

But it was a fiasco.

A doomed attempt: The dinghy began to take on water almost immediately. The traffickers swore in Arabic and for a while they kept going anyway. Then they stopped. "We're turning back," they told us. The end of the line, the end of our dreams and hopes.

"We were lucky to notice it early on, still close to the coast," they said. "If we were midway there we'd have sunk. We'd have all drowned." That's what they told us.

Only three hours.

Then back to Tripoli.

And nobody gives you your money back.

CHAPTER 29

※

NOW HERE I AM IN TRIPOLI, waiting; it's been two and a half months since we turned back. It's March 31, 2012. Only four months till the opening ceremony of the London Olympics and I know that I can still make it.

Three days after I returned to the apartment in the eastern outskirts of the city, a new girl arrived: Nigist, an Ethiopian. She was nervous, like all newcomers, but also elated: She had conquered the monster of the Sahara; she hadn't let it scare her. We became friends. She's like me: She's my same age and has the same build. If you ask me, we look alike, even though she says I'm prettier than she is. It's not true; I think she's prettier. I found her a place next to my mat. I didn't want her to end up in the clutches of some mean woman whose heart had been hardened by the Journey.

I went over my story a number of times with Nigist. She recognized me. She had seen me on TV nearly four years ago, at the

China Olympics, and since then, she says, she's never forgotten my face: my gentle, radiant smile, she says.

At first, like Abdullahi, she couldn't believe it was me. That I was there, like her, a *tahrib* like everyone else. A needy refugee. The second day she asked me. And I've never been more grateful to anyone. Nigist brought me back to life; that's why I decided to protect her. If she hadn't recognized me, I wouldn't have remembered who I was. It had been too long since I last looked in the mirror. The truth is that was something I didn't want to do. Whenever I happened to come near a reflective surface, I would avert my gaze. I hadn't seen my face in eight and a half months, except through the reactions of others when they looked at me.

That is why I will be forever grateful to Nigist. And why I like to tell her my story, again and again, almost every day. We must have had the same conversation—how many times? Twenty, thirty? Maybe more. Each time she asks me the same questions, or asks me new ones, and we find ourselves laughing at the same incidents. When Alì stole the candies that Aabe had saved for the feast of Eid, which marks the end of Ramadan, and as punishment Aabe made him eat them all, causing him to get diarrhea. When I ran in the stadium at night and imitated the noise of the crowd by taking a big breath and roaring: *aaaaarrghhhh*. When Alì fell into the big pool of excrement at the first race I won. When I told a reporter after the race in Beijing that I would have been happier if people had applauded me because I finished first and not last, and he'd burst out laughing in front of the TV camera. When Abdi actually thought that the aquarium in China was magical, and I confirmed it, and he fell for it. Then too the eucalyptus. When Alì climbed to the top and stayed there until he was weak from hunger. Like a monkey.

Another three months here in Tripoli without being able to leave the house for fear of being hounded by the police results in a lot of talking. There was a brief time, during the clashes and then right after the death of dictator Gadhafi at the end of 2011, when the situation was calmer. An absence of government means an absence of law. And without law even we *tahrib* were less *tahrib*. No one thought about us then because nobody was hunting us anymore. The traffickers were without work and a passage to Italy was cheap.

But now they've regrouped.

Worse than before. They say that if you, a *tahrib*, are found on the street, they'll send you straight back to the Sahara.

After I came back to Tripoli, I had to call Hodan and Hooyo again. But this would be the last money I'd ask for. This time, finally, I was going to make it.

I paid again, and here I am with Nigist, waiting for them to call and tell me it's time to leave. After you pay it's best to stay put in the house, because they could come at any time.

But now I've been told I'll leave tonight. This time they gave me a little advance notice, three hours, because the boat is big, they said, and there are a lot of us. My last three hours as a *tahrib*.

I'm used to departures: In eight months I've left at least six or seven times. I don't even have any bags to pack. Always the same three things: Aabe's headband, Hooyo's handkerchief with the seashell, the photo of Mo Farah.

Nigist and I will say good-bye when the time comes. Not before. During the Journey you don't do anything before you have to. There's no time for the past, there's no time for the future; only living in the present moment helps us survive, to stay alive. Practical things like good-byes don't fall into that category, so they are done only when the time comes.

Besides, we'll meet again later on; we've already talked about it.

Like me, Nigist too will come to live in Helsinki; we want to build a community of women from the Horn of Africa. Reproduce the colors of our countries in that distant, cold place.

I am very fond of Nigist; I'll miss her very much until we meet again.

Last night I spoke with Hodan via Skype, and with Mannaar as well. She's almost four years old, and by now it's clear that she looks exactly like me. There is a period, during the first two or three years as a child grows, when her appearance might take on any semblance whatsoever: She's not yet defined; she's just a sketch. By four years of age, however, she is what she was intended to be; she is already what she will be. Mannaar looks exactly like her aunt Samia. She resembles me more than she does her mother.

Hodan enrolled her at the gym a year ago.

She's been running for more than ten months now. Hodan was right about her; evidently mothers really do understand everything about their children, even before they are born. Mannaar has a flair for running; she's the fastest in her group. She has already won her first two races. And with those short little legs too. She's already so fast.

I'm her idol, that's what Hodan told me. One of the first words Mannaar uttered was "Tie Amia," Auntie Samia. She keeps my photograph—a newspaper clipping from the time of Beijing—next to her bed, as I did with Mo Farah's.

Each time I see her on Skype, I'm struck by how alike we are. Physically, two peas in a pod. But not only that. When she moves and talks, I feel like I'm seeing myself in miniature.

"Come soon," Mannaar told me last night. "Auntie Samia . . ." She paused. "Don't let the monsters come. . . . Don't say you're afraid."

Hodan and I both burst out laughing.

"No, little Mannaar, I'm not afraid. Ever," I told her.

Tonight I'm leaving at last.

It's time to leave; it's time to finally get there. I'm tired of this waiting. And tonight my aunt Mariam will also leave with me: She's one of Aabe's older sisters, whom I ran into by chance here in Tripoli when I went out to get the cans of water one day. She'd been living in an apartment nearby for nearly a month, and I didn't even know it.

She too was arrested three times during the Journey; she too is weary and needs a place where there's no war, a place from which you don't have to flee.

Tonight we leave and soon we'll find peace.

We'll find peace.

CHAPTER 30

✵

THE BOAT IS BIG, much bigger than I had imagined. It's an actual boat; the other one was a dinghy.

There are a great many of us, men, women, and children, from infants to the elderly; once more we seem like a crowd of excited, hopeful ghosts. There is no fear in our eyes; our gaze is focused far ahead, already looking beyond the sea.

We met at the port around eleven o'clock at night.

Aunt Mariam was there too. She's exhausted. She came with a woman friend with whom she made the Journey from Mogadishu. On the boat she found a place inside; I preferred to stay out on deck, to breathe in the smell of the sea, like a foretaste of the smell of freedom, the smell of Italy, of Europe.

The sea, the sea at last! It's the second time I'm seeing it up close like this. It's heaving slowly, gently, awaiting us.

There are about three hundred of us in all. Truly a great many. We make an impressive sight. Silent ghosts. The tremor in our bodies is a mixture of anxiety and hope. No one talks about it, because to talk about it would be to name one or the other. And naming things makes them real, so for tonight better not to. Better to keep anxiety locked up inside us and let hope grow, slowly perhaps, during the journey. Only then, only at the end, will we be able to rejoice, and do so all together. We'll weep and laugh together, and it will be wonderful. Like when we were in the trailer with the sacks of corn flour.

Not now, though; now is a time for silence. And prayer.

When they told us to board, we boarded.

Then we set off.

This time it's longer than the earlier three hours in the dinghy.

The voyage is smooth sailing, swift and steady. The sea is docile; our hull easily plows through it. Some sleep, others don't. I don't. I stay at the prow as long as I can to catch the breeze, until the cold becomes too intense and the night too dark. I stay there enjoying the wind and looking north, awaiting the land of freedom.

Then the first day is over.

We don't have much to eat, except for a little *angero* and *moffa*, a grain and corn flour mush. As usual, they haven't let us bring anything on board, because of weight. Not even water.

In fact, the water is all used up after a day and a half. A few try to say something; others even start shouting at the traffickers, but it's just to be doing something; it serves no purpose other than to mark time, going through the necessary motions that someone has to make.

After two days we're forced to drink water from the bottom of the boat's barrels. I would never have done it after the fever I caught in Khartoum, but I see that others are drinking it and not getting sick, so I drink it too. It's disgusting; it tastes of iron and urine. I find a small container and bring a little to Aunt Mariam, who must be thirsty.

"It's horrible," I tell her. "But it's all there is."

She's so dehydrated, her mouth parched, that she drinks it all in one gulp.

"Thank you, sweetheart," she replies in a faint whisper. Since they got on the boat, she and her friend haven't once moved from those seats. Lifeless, they sleep, pray, and eat what little the traffickers give us. They sit there, stock-still, staring out at the endless expanse of sea that separates us from freedom.

I go back inside to get some water for her friend as well.

Then I try to get some sleep outside in the sun during the day, because at night I like to watch the stars and I don't sleep. I may have rested just a couple of hours total; I'm too itchy with excitement. The sea conveys an energy I've never felt before; I've been waiting to see it since I was a little girl and went to glimpse it from afar with Alì and Hodan. I've been waiting for it a long time.

I keep to myself and don't speak to anyone. Suddenly a girl comes up to me, wanting to chat.

"Are you Somali?" she asks. As I had done with Taliya. I pretend I don't hear her. "Are you Somali?" she repeats. So I turn to her, nod my head "yes," and motion that I don't feel like talking. I want to be alone, just me, the sea, and the future. Just the three of us. Like me, Hodan and Alì, when we were little.

Then it happens.

Again. I can't believe it's really happening, but it happens.

Iblis, the devil, must have a hand in it, because the boat's engine fails. In the middle of the third day. May a thousand pounds of stinking shit fall on your heads, so fetid you'll never be able to wash away the stench.

We slow down and then stop.

I can't believe it. It can't be too much farther to the Italian coast. Yet we are stopped. We remain at a standstill for about fifteen hours.

Fifteen hours are endless if you know you are just a step away from the goal line. If, like me, you've been traveling for a year and a half, counting Addis Ababa. With the adrenaline I am producing, fifteen hours standing still is a time you can't even imagine. It's as if at the end of a race, just when there's one step left to go, one final stride to plow through the finish line, you were to run up against a transparent wall.

Some people have started raving. Others have begun calling upon Allah. The traffickers, all six of them, come down on deck and restore calm with the use of clubs. Shut up, *hawaian*!

"If you shout, for sure we won't get to Italy," they say.

After fifteen hours an Italian boat finally comes.

All together we begin waving our arms, jumping and singing, cheering, hopping up and down and jumping some more, and in the throes of a collective, uncontrollable euphoria, we all move to the same side, where the Italians are.

Some actually scramble up on the railing, wanting to jump into the water and swim out to the boat. With all the weight on one side, the boat is in danger of listing, of capsizing in the sea. Using a bullhorn, one of the traffickers shouts at us to return to our places.

Slowly almost everyone backs off, except a few who remain

clinging to the railing. Two already have their legs over the side, ready to jump.

Then we get it. Everything becomes clear.

They won't tow us, no.

Some are saying that they'll never rescue us and bring us to safety in Italy. We spend an hour like that, the two boats facing each other, maybe fifty yards apart, bobbing on the sea, the Italian captain speaking to our trafficker via radio.

On our boat, the rumor that they are going to bring us back circulates from ear to ear. They're going to call the Italian police and take us back to Tripoli. Or maybe Kufra. Some of us are terrified. Others depleted.

Someone starts shouting, "Noooo, you bastaaaaards!" at the top of his lungs, as if the sound of his voice could reach the Italian vessel. Instead it's lost somewhere amid the surging, increasingly angry waves.

Others move back to the rail again, threatening to jump with unmistakable gestures: They don't want to go back.

Then a decision is made on the Italian boat. The captain orders ropes to be thrown over the side, to be ready in case someone jumps.

The ropes hit the water with heavy plops, cutting cleanly through the towering, foamy waves crashing against the side of the vessel. There are about a dozen ropes in all. A dozen heavy plops, along the entire length of the hull.

Then it starts. It starts, and there's no going back.

A man from our floating wreck suddenly jumps into the sea. Without warning. No one could have anticipated it. The plop this time is much louder, as if a refrigerator has fallen in.

Everything halts, suspended; no one dares breathe a word. Time expands in that silence, on the brink. It's a state of waiting. Pure waiting. For something to happen. Whatever it is.

Very soon another man follows the first one.

Someone yells at him not to jump. "The sea is rough; the waves will swallow you," somebody else shouts.

Only at this point do a lot of us wake up and hurry over to the rail; the decrepit tub lists again.

Then yet another dives.

There's no way of knowing where the next person will jump from; everyone looks around to see if there will be another one. They look like fish dazzled by an intense, million-watt light, heads snapping left and right.

Now suddenly it's a woman who jumps.

No one can really believe it, but there are four people in the water who are struggling as hard as they can to reach the ropes. Two are swimming like mad, with broad, noisy strokes. The other two, including the woman, wrapped in veils that billow and swirl as she enters the water and resurfaces, are moving convulsively, their gestures spasmodic; it's clear to everyone that they don't know how to swim.

The water is choppy: It's an angry sea.

"Come back!" someone shouts.

"Don't be crazy; get back here!" somebody else yells.

Since the four bodies went into the sea, the waves seem even more towering, even rougher than before. I'm up against the rail like everyone else and I glance back at my aunt, who has come out on deck.

Then I look at the sea.

My sea.

She immediately understands and moves toward me.

Maybe it's written in my eyes, but somehow she understands.

"No!" is all she says.

"*Nooo!*" she says again.

She says it, but I can't hear her voice. I only see her lips moving.

Maybe I say something to her; maybe I tell her, "I'm not going back. Ever." But I'm not sure my voice really comes out.

Then a force greater than me makes me climb onto the rail. I don't know where it comes from; I don't know anything. It's that force that seizes me and makes me straddle the rail. It's not me, it's that force.

Aunt Mariam tries to tug me back, gripping my T-shirt, "Nooo! Samia, no!"

I swing one leg over.

Then the other.

Down below me is the sea. At last, the sea. And I can go in, and no one can stop me. For the first time in my life I can be embraced by all that water, I can swim in it, as I've always wanted to do.

Now I'm sitting on the edge of the rusty old tub, gazing at that infinite expanse, at the sea. I look at the ropes. I look at the sea.

I turn around.

I didn't even realize what I was doing. Aunt Mariam is behind me; she keeps pulling at my T-shirt and crying; I see her lips form a sound that I can't hear.

Then it happens. Again it happens.

I'm driven to life by this force that's seized me and decided to take me in hand.

It's a long way down, as every leap to freedom should be.

The water is icy cold and even rougher than it seemed from above.

I slice through the surface and reach the lowest point before the natural reascent. I open my eyes. There's a world of bubbles above me. There are slow, larger ones close to my head and small, very tiny ones racing swiftly toward the light, up to the surface. *Hsss hsss hsss hsss.* To my right and to my left, the dark shapes of the two vessels.

I thrust with my feet and rise back up. I emerge into the air and look around for the ropes.

I don't know which is our boat and which is the Italian one. I try to stay calm, while all around the sea is breaking over me, wave after wave.

The Italian boat is the one on the left.

I go under and come up, under and up. The water cradles me and takes hold of me. I swim a few vigorous strokes as forcefully as I can. I try to stay up and head for the ropes.

The ropes. The ropes are my goal, my finishing line.

As I slam my arms against the waves, I sing Hodan's song in my head: our song about freedom. I sing it to myself as I go under and come up; I try to sing it with my mouth but I can't, so I keep singing it in my mind.

Fly, Samia, fly, like a winged horse through the air. . . .

Dream, Samia, dream, like the wind playing among the leaves. . . .

Run, Samia, run, as if there were no particular reason. . . .

Live, Samia, live, as if everything were a miracle. . . .

. . .

. . .

. . .

Then, finally, something happens.

Someone grabs me by the hand and pulls me to the rope. I don't know how I do it, but thanks to this person whom I don't recognize but for whom I feel an infinite love, I manage to grasp the line. The contact with the water becomes more gentle, horizontal, now.

I'm swimming.

No, someone is pulling me up. They're lifting me on board the Italian boat.

. . . *Fly, Samia, fly, like a winged horse through the air.* . . .

Now I can breathe finally. I'm able to breathe.

Once I'm on board they'll take care of me.

They'll dry me and warm me up.

How nice to be warm; the sea is so cold.

After a short time, just a little while, not more than a few hours of sailing, we're in Lampedusa. In Italy.

It can't be true: I'm finally in Italy.

I realized my dream; I made it.

. . . *Dream, Samia, dream, like the wind playing among the leaves.* . . .

In Lampedusa I'm cared for.

They keep me in the hospital for two days. I tell them that I have to meet my coach in England, so they release me and take me to the airport.

From Lampedusa I take a plane to Rome.

From Rome another one to London.

In London, at Stansted, Mo Farah himself is waiting for me with his coach.

The first thing they do is complain about how long it took me to get there.

I apologize and we laugh; then all three of us head straight to the training field. I have a lot of time to make up, I know; I'm aware of it. I'll have to work hard.

I recover quickly; I respond well.

In a few weeks I'm as strong as I was before, even stronger than I was.

. . . Run, Samia, run, as if there were no particular reason. . . .

I just manage to make it in time to qualify for the 2012 London Olympics.

I'm in seventh heaven. I've never been more ecstatic.

I get through all the preliminary phases and, against all odds, make it to the finals.

The fans are with me.

On the starting blocks, televised worldwide, I'm in the fourth lane.

To my right is Veronica Campbell-Brown, to my left Florence Griffith Joyner, the fastest woman in the world.

. . . Live, Samia, live, as if everything were a miracle. . . .

Boom.

There's the start.

Now we run.

Samia Yusuf Omar died in the Mediterranean Sea on April 2, 2012, while trying to reach ropes tossed out from an Italian vessel.

At the 2012 London Olympics, Mo Farah won the five-thousand- and ten-thousand-meter races, becoming a national hero in England and Somalia. A picture of him with Usain Bolt was viewed around the globe: the world's swiftest sprinter and strongest long-distance runner in the same photograph.

Mannaar is five years old and still looks a lot like her aunt. It seems she is one of the fastest girls her age.

Samia

Mannaar. Helsinki, February 2013.

ACKNOWLEDGMENTS

THIS BOOK IS THE RESULT of the efforts of a great many people—those who in various ways helped me write it or played a part in improving it once written or, even before that, gave me needed support to find the determination to write it.

First of all, thanks to my parents, who have always been there for me and who are a mainstay at even the most difficult moments, times when you're not sure which way to go. Thanks to my *nonna* Michelina, who I know is smiling down from somewhere, watching me as I tap this keyboard. A big thanks to everyone at the Feltrinelli publishing house. Thanks to Carlo Feltrinelli for having loved the project from the start. Thanks to Gianluca Foglia for wanting to see it realized and for taking such care with it. Thanks to Alberto Rollo for having played a role in developing the emotional sensibility in me to "hear" Samia's voice and for having been the first to tell me, "It's beautiful." Thanks to Alessandro Monti for his attentive, profound words after reading the book. Thanks to Giovanna Salvia for her invaluable work on the text. Thanks to Chiara Cardelli and Bettina Cristiani for having caught many things that still weren't right. Thanks to Theo Collier and Bianca Dinapoli for having promoted this story to so many people around the world. Thanks to Alberto Schiavone, one of the first whom I let read this book. A collective thanks to Francesca Cappennani, Annalisa Laborai, Silvia Cassoni, Benedetta Bellisario, Rossella Fancoli, Francisco Lopez, and Ludovica Piccardo and Agnese Radaelli of the Association *Il Razzismo è una brutta storia* for agreeing to read the first draft and for the enthusiasm they expressed to me. Thanks to Andrea Vigentini and Salvatore Panaccione for their words, on more than one occasion. Thanks to Rodolfo Montuoro for his support and energy throughout. Thanks to Rosie Ficocelli for her precision on each of the drafts. Thanks to Raf Scelsi, who was able to listen at times when I was at a loss. Thanks to Giulia Romano, who shared many talks with me. Thanks to Gomma for the constant encouragement from afar. Thanks to Ana Díaz Ramírez for the photo. Thanks to Cristiano Guerri and Duccio Boscoli for all the work I made them do on the cover.

A huge thank-you also goes to my agent, Roberto Santachiara, a pillar of support and the second person ever with whom I shared this story, for having immediately encouraged me to write it.

Thanks to Roberto Saviano for having told me at what for me was a difficult moment: "Write!"

Thanks again to Igiaba Scego, with whom it all started.

Thanks to Francesco Polimanti for being responsive and open

during the talk I gave about Samia's story at the University of Miami in October 2013.

Thanks to someone who is always there for me: my sister Nicoletta.

And finally, my thanks to Chiara: There's no need to reveal here how much you helped me before, during, and after.

AUTHOR'S NOTE

I CAME UPON THE STORY of Samia Yusuf Omar by chance, on August 19, 2012, in Lamu, Kenya. It was morning, and Al Jazeera's news report had briefly mentioned her at the conclusion of the London Olympics. The story struck me. A few days later I returned to Italy, where the writer Igiaba Scego had written about it in *Pubblico*. It is thanks to Igiaba and to Zahra Omar, far more than a mediator and interpreter, that I was able to meet Hodan and Mannaar in Helsinki during the frigid February of 2013. It is thanks to Zahra that Hodan and I were able to communicate in what immediately seemed like the same language. It is only thanks to Igiaba and to Zahra, therefore, that this book exists.

I can never thank Hodan enough for those lengthy talks during endless days of seclusion in a hotel room, for her tears and sobs, for her laughter and her songs, and for giving me the courage and strength to tell her sister's story. My gratitude to her for having entrusted me with this story, which I hope I have been able to re-create in some small way at least. And my thanks for the delicious Somali food that she brought me at the hotel when every restaurant nearby was closed.

Thanks also to Mannaar, who in the hours we spent together filled me with energy and vitality.

I also want to thank the young woman who in the book is called Nigist—who wishes to remain nameless, still afraid of what the Libyan police could do to her if they found her—for telling me about her endless conversations with Samia in the thirty days they spent together in Tripoli, in the same house with forty other women.

TRANSLATOR'S NOTE

❉

THIS IS A MOVING STORY about an extraordinary, spirited young woman. We first meet Samia in the setting of her childhood years, where two Somali families—hers and that of her childhood "brother" Alì—share meager rented quarters. Their courtyard with its giant eucalyptus tree is an island of normality in a country racked by poverty and brutal warring among clans, and it is these conditions that Samia is determined to overcome.

A word about the time line. Samia was born March 25, 1991, in Mogadishu, Somalia, and died August 19, 2012, in the Mediterranean. The narrative opens in 1999, when Samia and her best friend, Alì, are eight years old. By 2005, when Alì and his family are driven to move away, Samia is fourteen. In 2008 Samia travels to China to represent Somalia at the Summer Olympics in Beijing. When she turns twenty in 2011, she undertakes the long, harrowing Journey out of Somalia, hoping to eventually take part in the London Olympics in 2012. She drowns at sea trying to reach Italy in 2012, at twenty-one years of age.

The setting of the novel—the war-torn country of Somalia and, in particular, Samia's beloved Mogadishu—acts as a character in its own right, the nemesis that Samia both loves and opposes and from which she is forced to reluctantly flee.

Born the same year Major General Mohamed Siad Barre was overthrown as president of Somalia and the government collapsed, Samia grows up with war as an "older sister." Barre had ruled the impoverished country for more than twenty years, after seizing power in 1969 and establishing the Somali Democratic Republic. Under his dictatorship Somalia had been a relatively stable nation. Barre's government collapsed in 1991 as civil war broke out. His departure from the scene (preceding his death in exile in Nigeria in 1995) left Somalia without a central authority and with a government in disarray: Chaos broke out as local warlords battled for territory. As civil war raged among feuding clans and their militias, municipal services ceased and the country was left on the brink of destruction, with no food, no clean water, and no power. In a city where the parched soil had crumbled to white dust and ruins dominate the landscape, the atmosphere was one of inevitability.

Despite the inexorable bleakness and despair, the indignity, violence, and loss, Samia's determination thrives and a mood of hopefulness prevails throughout her early life. The setting of her childhood years—the two families living around the eucalyptus tree, Samia and her childhood "brother" Alì promising that nothing will ever come between them—is an oasis of calm, an island of normality, in a country racked by poverty and brutal warring among clans. Only when she eventually embarks on the Journey to escape the jagged circumstances of her homeland does Samia's single-minded, hopeful optimism desert her.

It is on her journey to freedom that Samia becomes an outcast, an exiled refugee, or *tahrib*, who is ostracized from human society. The process of dehumanization begins in Ethiopia, in Addis Ababa, before she even starts the Journey, when she is forced to watch the other athletes practice from behind a wire mesh fence outside the stadium: "I remained a *tahrib*, running alone." As the Journey drags on, the process of marginalization intensifies to the point where she is no longer able to remember who she was before. By the time she reaches Sudan, the traffickers are referring to their downtrodden charges as *hawaian*, animals.

When I finished reading the book, I was left wondering what had become of Alì, Samia's onetime "brother" and "coach." I asked Giuseppe Catozzella whether he had ever tried to find Alì when he was doing his research for the book. I knew he had spoken at length with Hodan, Samia's sister, but I wondered if he'd been able to speak with Alì or knew where he might be now. I thought a brief word from this individual who is so central to Samia's story might make a wonderful afterword to the narrative. Giuseppe was quick to introduce a note of reality, explaining that circumstances in Somalia made it impossible to trace Alì. He added that the latest word is that Alì is still in Somalia, although no one has seen him in years.

I also asked Giuseppe if he had copies of any of the letters that Samia read during the time she spent in prison in Ajdabiya. The text reads: "Pray, wait, and read. In fact there were letters in that prison. In Arabic, in Somali, in Ethiopian, and in English, left there somehow, for some reason, tossed aside in a corner, accumulated over years and years. Letters from prisoners or from their loved ones. Maybe they were mementos of the dead that the guards had never had the nerve to discard. In those letters there were lives. And so, reading them, I rediscovered what no longer existed inside of me. Life. Memories. Love. Promises. Courage. Hope."

Throughout it all, the young woman with the resilience of a survivor remains stubbornly anchored to her family and her homeland, and though she leaves them, it is with the hope of pursuing her goal and finding her way back. All in all, Samia's story of hope and aspiration, written with the passionate urgency of a firsthand account, is an affecting narrative with truly wrenching, very moving moments.

Anne Milano Appel

GLOSSARY

❋

aabe: father

abaayo: sister

aboowe: brother

angero: a type of crepe

aroos: wedding celebration

buraanbur: Somali women's poetry that expresses happiness or sadness in times of war or as a celebration of life

burgico: brazier

garbasar: shawl

gobeys: a kind of flute

griir: a game played by tossing pebbles

hawiye: militiamen, affiliated with Abgal

hooyo: mother

kaban: lute

kirisho mirish: a type of spicy meat and rice dish (Samia's favorite)

koor: the bell a camel wears around its neck

niiko: Somali music danced to during weddings

qamar, hijab, diric: Islamic veils worn by women

shaat: a type of tea drink

shambal: a musical instrument consisting of two pieces of wood with a hole in the middle

shareero: a string instrument; a type of lyre

shentral: a board game

wiilo: tomboy